The
Army Doctor's
New Year's Baby

Helen Scott Taylor

Other Books in the Army Doctor's Series

Acknowledgments

Thanks go to my wonderful critique partner Mona Risk who is always there when I need her help, to my son Peter Taylor for creating a gorgeous book cover, and, as always, to my reliable editor Pam Berehulke.

Chapter One

Major Daniel Fabian's breath misted before him in the cold as he strolled along Park Lane in London's fashionable Mayfair district. Black cabs whizzed past, ferrying New Year's Eve revelers to parties while Christmas lights glittered among the icy branches of the trees in Hyde Park.

This was Daniel's first time wearing dress uniform since he'd graduated from the Royal Military Academy Sandhurst six months ago. Satisfaction filled him at the respectful glances from people he passed. He was proud to be a member of the British Army Medical Corps, proud to be part of an organization that provided a service for his country.

Too much of his life had been wasted on the wrong career and pointless relationships with women he didn't care about. Now he had turned over a new leaf. His New Year's resolution was to make a worthy contribution to the army, to forge a future he could be proud of.

He reached his destination and joined the other guests in army uniform heading through the front entrance of the Dorchester Hotel for the Royal Army Medical Corps' New Year's Eve Ball.

As he stepped through the door, his new commanding officer approached as if he'd been lying in wait. "Major Fabian, thank goodness you're here. Can I ask you a huge favor?" Col. Duncan Mackenzie dragged a worried hand over his dark hair. "Would you escort my sister, Megan, into the ballroom? I forgot I was supposed to do it. Now I've committed to take another woman in."

Daniel suppressed an ironic smile. He'd pledged to devote himself to the army during his first year of military service, with no distractions of the female kind. Yet every time he attended a social function, people tried to hook him up with a woman.

Despite his reluctance, he had no intention of turning down Colonel Mackenzie's request. He didn't want to start off on the wrong foot with him. "I'd be delighted to, sir."

"I'll call Meg and see where she is." Duncan pulled a mobile phone from the sporran hanging over the front of his kilt and held it to his ear.

"Hey, Dan, how are you doing?" Two young doctors who'd been in Daniel's class at Sandhurst stopped to chat about their first postings.

They had both joined the army straight out of medical school. Daniel envied them for having no doubts about what they wanted to do. He'd wasted eight years working as a cosmetic surgeon in his father's exclusive London clinic before he found the strength to leave and go his own way. His father hadn't spoken to him since.

"Right, Meg's coming down," Duncan said. "We'll meet her by the elevator."

Daniel followed the Scotsman through the milling crowd in the reception area. Standing at just over six feet it was rare he felt small, but the colonel's tall, burly frame dwarfed him.

As they approached the elevator, the door slid open. A group of attractive women in evening dress stepped out. The blonde and brunette he hadn't met but recognized as the wives of Radley and Cameron Knight. The small woman with bright red hair in an elegant side-swept chignon must be the colonel's sister. A tartan sash made of the same fabric as Duncan's kilt draped across her long green dress.

"We're off to tear our husbands away from the bar. See you inside," the brunette said to Megan, then she and the blonde left.

Megan Mackenzie's attention moved to Duncan. She pinned him with a look that left no doubt who was boss in the Mackenzie household. The Scotsman dutifully bent and kissed her cheek.

"You look bonnie tonight, Meg."

Her eyes narrowed. "What have you done wrong?"

Duncan cleared his throat. "Can't I compliment my sister without an ulterior motive?"

She pressed her bright red lips together, creases appearing between her eyebrows. "You forgot you were my partner again, didn't you?"

"I'm sorry, Meg. Colonel Maitland asked me to escort his daughter. I agreed without thinking."

"Oh, Duncan. Every year you do this to me." Lines of irritation bracketed her mouth, her full lips pursed, signaling her displeasure. She was a tiny thing, her face fine-boned, her skin pale, a smattering of freckles across her nose and arms.

Although pretty, she was not the sort of woman Daniel dated. He wasn't quite sure what to make of her.

"Don't worry," Duncan said. "Major Fabian will walk you in."

Duncan glanced his way and Megan's gaze followed, pink staining her cheeks. She examined him with warm brown eyes flecked with green and gold. As their eyes met, something inside Daniel flipped over with a bump that momentarily fogged his brain.

"Major Fabian, meet my baby sister, Megan

Mackenzie."

"Not so much of the baby, thank you, Duncan. Anyone would think I was still in diapers."

A smile caught Daniel's lips. She had the most adorable soft Scottish brogue and enough attitude to cut a man down to size—even a colonel.

"It's a pleasure to meet you, Miss Mackenzie."

"It's Dr. Mackenzie, actually. My brother might believe I exist solely to keep house for him, but I don't."

She held out her hand. Daniel gripped her slender fingers. She squeezed back, shaking firmly as if they were sealing a business deal. Megan Mackenzie had a confident, capable air that belied her fragile appearance. She was rather like the little terrier he'd owned as a boy that always put his brother's Alsatian in its place.

"I take your career very seriously, Meg," Duncan said, a note of frustration in his voice that hinted at a long-running disagreement.

Megan turned to answer someone who greeted her and Duncan angled his head towards Daniel, speaking out of the corner of his mouth. "I wouldn't dare do otherwise."

Megan's gaze jumped back to them. "I heard that, Duncan Mackenzie." She placed a hand beneath his elbow and pushed him on his way. "Off you go to find this woman who is more important than me."

Duncan gave her a pained look, but didn't argue. He simply did as he was told. Nodding at Daniel, he headed off into the crowd.

When Duncan had disappeared, Megan turned her gaze on Daniel. He grinned; he couldn't help himself. For a few moments, her lips flattened as if she were determined to be annoyed, then she gave up and smiled, her eyes sparkling.

"I apologize that you've been stuck with me, Major Fabian. I appreciate your willingness to step in for my brother, but if you have other obligations, I'm capable of walking into the ballroom alone." She dropped her gaze, looking down to straighten her tartan sash. She was obviously embarrassed to be foisted on him. Maybe she wasn't quite as confident as she pretended?

A feeling stole through him—an unfamiliar desire to ease this woman's discomfort and make her feel valued.

"You'll do me a service if you allow me to escort you inside. I came alone as well." Although Daniel had no problem with his single status, Megan didn't need to know that.

"Oh." She glanced at him again, her self-assurance revived. "Well, thank you, Major Fabian. I'll be delighted to walk in with you."

Daniel held out his elbow for Megan to slip her hand through. She rested her slender fingers on his forearm. They joined the crowd in army uniform approaching the ballroom.

Her nails were painted bright red, matching her lips and the stripe in her tartan. He nodded towards her sash. "Is that the Mackenzie plaid?"

"It is, and this is our coat of arms." She touched a brooch holding the sash in place on her shoulder. "A blessing and a curse," she added softly, as if to herself.

"I rather like the idea of having a family heritage and a coat of arms. My family has nothing like that." In fact, his family was falling apart at the seams. He hadn't spoken to his father for nearly a year, and now his mother had gone off with another man. Apart from his brother, Sean, the army was all he had.

"Being the laird's daughter carries with it obligations and expectations that make life difficult. Even in this day and age it means I can't marry just anyone. I fear it might be my destiny to keep house for my brothers for the rest of my life."

Her gaze flicked up to him and away, pink tingeing her cheeks. "Forgive me, Major. I'm sure you don't want to listen to me complaining."

Normally when women talked about relationship problems, Daniel switched off. Yet Megan Mackenzie's lifestyle sounded so different from his own that it interested him. He wanted to keep her talking.

"You have such a lovely voice, everything you say is music to my ears." Daniel winced inwardly the moment the flattery slipped out—a habit so ingrained, he spoke without thinking. He knew instinctively Megan would not appreciate that type of comment.

She flashed him a disbelieving glance, then burst out laughing. "Do women really fall for lines like that?"

"Some do," he admitted ruefully. "Although it's true, I love listening to your accent."

Her blush deepened. She looked down, but not before he caught her smiling to herself.

They reached the entrance to the ballroom and paused to stare over the spectacular room with its chandeliers and mirrored walls, the décor rich gold and blue tones.

In a few minutes, they'd arrive at her table and he'd have to give her up. He didn't want to. It would be a pleasure to spend more time with Megan.

"Do you know where you're seated?" He hoped there was a chance they might sit together.

Her speculative gaze lingered on his face for a few moments. "I won't know until after the auction."

"They auction the seats?" That didn't make sense. People were already sitting at the tables.

Her soft, melodic laughter rang out as she shook her head. "You're obviously a first timer if you don't know the drill. They auction the women."

Daniel had been to such events in his former life, glamorous occasions where high society women took part to raise funds for charity. He'd always found it an amusing diversion, but the thought of Megan going to the highest bidder put his back up.

"It's only for fun. Men bid on the woman they want to dine with. It's simply a way of raising money for the Heroes' Kids Fund that supports the children of servicemen who die in action. They do very well from the auction and everyone enjoys the evening."

The nervous undertone in her voice belied her reassuring words. She wasn't any more comfortable with this than he was. He led her out of the crowd to the side of the room and moved in front of her, shielding her from view. "You don't have to take part in the auction if you don't want to. I'll go and tell whoever's organizing it that you've withdrawn."

He had the irrational urge to take her hand and walk out, retreat with her to a quiet restaurant where they could dine together in peace.

"Thank you for your concern, but I'm fine." She gave a small smile. "My brother Blair runs the charity, so I have to take part." She nodded towards the far end of the room where a group of women was gathering. "I need to join them. Dinner will start soon."

Daniel walked her down the side of the ballroom. Her fingers stiffened against his arm as they approached the stage. He placed his hand over hers and squeezed in silent support. Her gaze rose to his, grateful and a little haunted. Something jolted in his chest as if his heart had jumped and turned over.

What was it about Megan Mackenzie that got to him? These feelings were unfamiliar.

They reached the edge of the chattering group of women. Daniel gave her up with a large dose of reluctance. After such a short time in her company, it was amazing how possessive he felt about this woman.

"Thank you for walking me in, Daniel. I appreciate it. Maybe I'll see you again sometime."

"I hope so."

Daniel stood for a few moments, searching for something more to say, not wanting to leave. He had to consciously turn away to break the spell this unusual woman had cast over him. He wandered back towards his table, glancing over his shoulder to where the auction candidates were lining up. With her old-fashioned tartan sash, Megan looked small, vulnerable, and strangely out of place among the fashion parade of glamorous females. He wanted her to sit beside him during dinner. It screwed up his no-women pledge, but this was just one evening. Surely that wouldn't hurt?

Chapter Two

Megan tore her glance from Daniel Fabian's retreating back with a little sigh of longing and edged towards her friends through the excited group of women who were waiting for the auction to start.

Olivia Knight raised her elegant eyebrows as Megan approached. "You're a dark horse. I didn't realize you knew Sean's brother."

Megan laughed. "I don't, really. My brother rather dropped him in it. Daniel was too much of a gentleman to refuse to escort me."

Olivia's expression grew serious. "Sean's told us lots of tales about Daniel's busy social life. Apparently he was a cosmetic surgeon to the stars before he joined the army. He doesn't sound like a settling-down sort of guy. Do be careful. I'd hate to see you hurt."

Secretly, Megan would love the opportunity to get close enough to the gorgeous Daniel Fabian to risk being hurt. But that was unlikely to happen. Men with Daniel's looks did not date parochial doctors with ginger hair and freckles who lived in the middle of the Scottish Highlands.

She glanced over her shoulder to see Daniel talking to a tall, willowy woman with masses of mahogany hair. They were laughing together, obviously friends if not more. No, Megan stood no chance with him at all.

"Actually, I rather like him, and he is easy on the eye." Alice Knight grinned. "He's sitting at our table. It

9

would be great if he bids on you, Meg. Then we'll all be able to sit together."

Megan's brother Blair came up behind Olivia and Alice and put his arms around their shoulders. "Do I hear you three plotting? Don't tell me you Knights have fixed the auction again."

He kissed Alice's and Olivia's cheeks then hugged Megan, lifting her off her feet like he had ever since she was a little girl. "Behave yourselves, ladies, and have fun. We're about to start. Talk to you shortly."

He headed back to the stage and called for everyone's attention. The lights glinted off his shiny dark hair, his smile bright, his eyes twinkling with enthusiasm. He was passionate about his charity for children who'd lost parents to conflict.

"Ladies and gentlemen, please take your seats for the charity auction to benefit the Heroes' Kids Fund." He turned and extended a hand. "These beautiful women are looking for dinner partners to share the evening with. So be ready to dig deep in your pockets as the bidding is about to start."

A pretty young woman with silky blonde hair and blue eyes stepped up first.

Blair grinned at her and took her hand. "Miss Charlotte Maitland tells me she likes vampires, so if you know anything about vampires, this is the girl for you."

"Does Dracula count," a male voice shouted from the back, making everyone laugh.

"Who will start the bidding? Am I bid fifty pounds?"

Male hands shot up all over the ballroom. The price rapidly rose to seven hundred pounds until she was sold to a young officer Megan didn't know.

Three more women went up. The bidding continued, then Alice Knight stepped up beside Blair, delicate and pretty, her blonde hair caught back in diamante clips, her blue satin dress emphasizing her slim figure.

A couple of bids came from the front of the room, then Alice's husband, Cameron Knight, stood. "One thousand pounds," he announced in a tone of finality. Before Blair even declared the auction over, Cameron was already threading his way between the tables to claim his wife.

He handed her down the stairs, then kissed her to a round of applause before he led her back to their table.

Next, Olivia Knight joined Blair on the stage, stunning in a burgundy dress with a diamond and ruby necklace and matching bracelet. Her long dark hair flowed loose down her back. She was so elegant and self-assured, confident in the knowledge that her man loved her and would bid whatever it took to spend his evening with her.

A little sigh whispered between Megan's lips, and she pushed away a stab of envy. How she wished she could find a loving husband like her friends.

The bidding started quickly, rapidly reaching a thousand pounds. At that point, Radley Knight rose to his feet. The room fell silent as if no one else dared challenge a colonel, now that he'd made his intentions clear. "Two thousand pounds," he said in ringing tones as he headed towards the stage.

"That's about five hundred quid an hour," someone shouted, raising a laugh from the crowd.

"And worth every penny," Radley quipped as he claimed his wife's hand to lead her back to their table.

Blair turned, his gaze finding Megan. He nodded and the young officer who was assisting handed her up the stairs.

"Now I have the pleasure of presenting my lovely sister, Dr. Megan Mackenzie. What am I bid to spend the evening with a bonnie Scottish lass?"

Although Megan willed herself not to blush, her cheeks heated. It was a curse of her coloring that she did not blush well. She pasted on a smile and kept her hands still, resisting the urge to fiddle with her sash.

Blair continued. "We army doctors think we know about danger, but if you want to hear some hairy stories of rescuing casualties from dangerous situations, this is your girl. Megan works with mountain rescue in the Scottish Highlands."

"Five hundred pounds." Major General Knight's baritone boomed deep and clear through the momentary silence in the ballroom. She'd known good old Uncle George all her life; he was one of her father's best friends. She could always count on him to start the bidding on her.

"Six hundred," another man said, although she didn't catch who.

"Seven hundred," Uncle George countered.

Silence fell and Megan's heart beat a rapid tattoo in her chest. This was the truly nerve-wracking part of the auction, standing up in front of 250 people praying for bids.

She'd made a conscious effort not to look at Daniel, but now her gaze skated over the upturned faces in search of blonde hair, blue eyes, and a warm smile.

He sat at the table with her friends, an empty seat beside him. Her breath caught; for a moment she struggled to suck in air. The woman Daniel had been talking to was not with him, she was seated next to his brother, Sean.

Daniel leaned back in his chair, a lazy smile on his face as he watched the proceedings. She tore her gaze away from him and let it drift unseeing over the mass of people. Her chest ached with longing—if only he would bid on her. When the clock struck twelve tonight and kisses were exchanged to celebrate the New Year, she wanted to be sitting beside Daniel Fabian.

The bidding continued. Another of her father's friends offered nine hundred pounds for her, then silence fell. Megan consciously drew in a breath and pushed it out, her heartbeat marking off the seconds. Any moment now, Blair would declare her sold.

Her fingers flexed on her purse, crushing the soft fabric. Much as she appreciated her father's friends supporting her, it was humiliating to be passed over by the younger men. They all probably had their sights set on the pretty young daughters of the senior officers who were still waiting in line.

"Three thousand pounds." The words echoed around the room. Clothes rustled and chairs scraped as everyone turned to see who had bid such a large amount.

Daniel rose, the lights glinting off his blond hair. Giving the impression he enjoyed the limelight, he stepped behind his brother's chair and ambled between the tables, obviously in no hurry, a self-assured smile on his face.

"Sold to Major Fabian," Blair announced. There was a moment's stunned silence, then applause broke out and rippled through the crowd.

Megan trembled, her legs suddenly unsteady. She gripped Blair's arm for support as he led her to the top of the steps. "Way to go, Meggie," he said under his breath. "Highest bid of the night by far."

Then louder he said, "Major Fabian has set the bar high, gentlemen. Let's see if we can top his generous donation before the night is out." He passed Meg's hand to Daniel and stepped back.

Daniel glanced up at her, his blue eyes twinkling with pleasure. "Will you join me, Dr. Mackenzie?"

Despite the mad jig of her heart and wobbly knees, somehow she hung on to her composure. "I'd be delighted to, Major Fabian."

His warm fingers gripped hers to guide her slowly down the stairs and back between the tables.

Alice grinned as Daniel pulled out the chair for Meg. "Wonderful. I'm so pleased you're at our table."

Radley and Cameron Knight both greeted her with a hug and a kiss on the cheek. They had been at school with her brothers and she'd known them all her life.

Daniel introduced her to his brother, Sean, who sat on her left with his wife, Kelly, the woman with the mahogany hair.

She placed her purse on the table and waited until the auction recommenced, then leaned towards Daniel. "Thank you for rescuing me again," she said softly.

"It's my pleasure." His fingers brushed the back of her hand, the lightest of caresses, but she felt that touch in every fiber of her being.

Her heart fluttered like a moth in a bottle. What was it about this man that had her in a spin? It wasn't just his good looks, although they helped.

She tried to concentrate on the auction, clapping politely after each woman was sold, yet most of her attention focused on the gorgeous man at her side as if her body had realigned itself to his wavelength.

She adored the Scottish Highlands, adored the rugged wild countryside, the mountains, the snow, and the wildlife. But at this moment, she wished with all her heart she lived closer to civilization, closer to where Daniel lived. She longed for the chance to get to know him better. But that would never happen.

Her responsibilities, her mountain rescue work, and everything that mattered to her were in Scotland and always would be.

She must make the most of her few hours with Daniel, because they might be all she ever had.

The evening passed in a blur of happy conversation and laughter as Megan caught up with the news about her friends' children. Sean Fabian and his wife, Kelly, had adopted a six-week-old baby boy just before Christmas. Kelly passed her mobile phone around to show off photos of their three children.

After the main course of dinner, Sean and Kelly

wished everyone a happy New Year and left before dessert, so eager were they to be home with their new baby, Liam, and their twin girls.

Whenever she could, Megan snatched moments of private conversation with Daniel. He asked her about her work with Kindrogan Mountain Rescue. She related some of the most dangerous rescues to impress him.

"So tell me, how do you know Duncan?" Megan felt as though she had been talking about herself all evening. It was time she found out more about Daniel.

He glanced down and straightened his napkin, the light shining off the paler streaks in his blond hair. "I met him at a medical conference in Canada a few years ago, before I joined the army. His work on freezing-cold injury interests me." He paused for a second as if thinking, then met her gaze with a slightly strained smile. Was he uncomfortable talking about himself?

"His line of work has personal relevance for me. I'm a bit of a snowboarding junkie. I trained as an instructor between school and college and passed my level two. It gave me the chance for lots of riding freestyle, off-piste, and backcountry."

"And plenty of après ski as well, I imagine," Megan added, hoping to turn the conversation to his social life. She didn't really want to hear about all the girlfriends Olivia had hinted at, but at the same time she did want to know what sort of man Daniel was.

At that moment, the lights dimmed and the band that had set up on the stage started playing. A number of couples stood and stepped onto the small dance floor in the center of the room.

"Would you do me the honor?" Daniel said, rising and holding out his hand. She had the impression he was avoiding talking about himself, but she often overanalyzed things. Relax and enjoy the evening, she told herself.

Daniel's arms came around her, strong and warm.

As he eased her into his embrace, her rational thoughts slipped away. She drifted into a dreamy heaven against his chest, imagining he was really hers and he cared about her. She had known him for only a few hours, yet already she was halfway in love with him.

She leaned her head on his shoulder and breathed in the spicy smell of his aftershave as the singer crooned. They circled the dance floor with the other couples, enjoying the strange intimacy of being in each other's arms amid the crowd. She could not imagine a better way to bring in the New Year.

Daniel seemed in no hurry to sit down again. They danced together for at least an hour, swaying to the rhythm. She wished the evening could go on forever, but eventually the music ended and her brother Blair stepped up to the microphone. "Charge your glasses, ladies and gentlemen. It's five minutes to twelve."

Daniel took her hand and led her back to their table, where fresh flutes of champagne waited for them. He picked up hers and handed it over, then lifted his own. Blair started a countdown as the chimes of Big Ben were broadcast into the ballroom. Everyone joined in, cheering when they reached midnight.

"Happy New Year!" Blair shouted over the joyful hubbub as people congratulated each other.

Daniel tapped his glass against hers. "Here's to new beginnings," he said. Then he set down his drink and drew Megan into his arms.

Her heart thundered and she could barely draw breath.

"Happy New Year, sweetheart," he whispered as he held her close. She melted into his arms, resting her palms against his shoulders. He bent his head and his lips brushed hers in a sweet kiss that was over far too soon.

Then he released her and turned away, kissing Olivia and Alice, shaking hands with Radley and

16

Cameron. Her mind fuzzy, her breath short as if she were standing on a high mountain peak where the air was thin, Megan shared good wishes with the others, kissing Radley and Cameron, hugging Alice and Olivia, all chatting with excitement.

Even as she laughed with her friends, her attention was really on Daniel, her ears attuned to the pleasant timbre of his voice, her fingers aching to sink into the warm grip of his hand.

When he turned back to her, his arm slipping around her waist, sensation zinged along her nerves. Daniel's touch made her feel more alive than she'd ever felt before.

She didn't want this night to end. She didn't want to say good-bye to him.

"Are you staying in the hotel?" he asked.

"Yes. Duncan and Blair are too."

He'd already told her he lived in London, so he'd be returning home tonight for his last week of leave before his new posting. When she inquired where he was being sent, he'd been a little mysterious and hadn't answered.

"Shall we go outside to catch the end of the firework display over the River Thames? We should be able to see some of them from here."

"Oh, yes. Good idea." Anything to extend the evening.

Megan's cheeks were warm, her head light from the champagne. Daniel took her hand and led her into the reception area. He slipped off his jacket, draping it over her shoulders. "It'll be chilly outside. I don't want you to get cold."

"What about you?"

"Real men don't feel the cold. Didn't you know?"

She laughed as he led her out the main door. "Real men feel the cold in Scotland, Daniel. Believe me."

They crossed the road to Hyde Park and stared into

the sky, catching the last few minutes of the massive pyrotechnic display over London to celebrate the New Year.

When the fireworks finished, Daniel took her hand. They wandered beneath the lit-up trees, frost forming spiderwebs of ice on the grass and plants. Megan shivered, more from excitement than cold. Had he brought her out here to kiss her again?

"There's something I need to tell you." The serious tone of Daniel's voice sent a frisson of unease through her.

"My next posting is in Scotland." Daniel cast Megan a sideways glance.

He was going to be posted near her home? Why did he sound so glum about it?

"I'll be working with Duncan at the Army Institute of Survival and Thermal Medicine."

For a moment, she couldn't breathe. She'd imagined she wouldn't see Daniel again for months, but he would be stationed six miles from where she lived.

Turning to face him, she gripped his hand in both of hers. "Daniel, that's wonderful. We can see each other again." His frown dampened her excitement. "Is something wrong?"

"Duncan asked me if I'd like to stay with him."

Megan's already pounding heart nearly burst out of her chest. Daniel was coming to stay at Kindrogan Castle? She would have been over the moon if not for the lines of tension on his face.

"Before I accept his offer, I want to check that it's okay with you."

Was the man crazy? Didn't he realize how much she liked him?

"It'll be lovely to have you to stay." Megan nearly bit her tongue, she spit her words out so fast.

"The thing is, I don't want to give you the wrong impression. It's only fair to make it clear up front that

I'm not looking for a romantic relationship."

Her heart crashed, the avalanche of disappointment sending a shockwave along her nerves. Did he mean he didn't want a romantic relationship at all, or was he just not interested in her?

Megan turned away and stared at a red double-decker bus trundling along the road. Why was she surprised? Men were never attracted to her. Not men like Daniel, anyway. She had been a fool to imagine, even for a nanosecond, that he might be.

Blinking away tears, she summoned a stoic expression. Rejections too numerous to recall had taught her how to put on a brave face. She swallowed hard and cleared her throat, then turned back towards him. "That's not a problem. You're still welcome to stay with Duncan. We can be friends, can't we?"

"Of course. I'd like that. I've really enjoyed our evening together. It's nothing to do with you, Meg. It's me."

Stop, please stop, she mentally entreated him. After the lovely evening they'd shared, he was ruining it.

"I promised myself I'd concentrate on the army for twelve months with no distractions." He gave a wry laugh. "I've been far too easily distracted by women in the past."

Meg looked down and fiddled with her purse. Tears pricked the back of her eyes and clogged her throat. She had to get away from Daniel before she cried all over him. She'd never be able to face him when he came to stay if that happened.

Shivering, she hugged her arms around herself. "I'm chilly. I'm going inside."

"Of course. Sorry to drag you out here, but I wanted to talk in private."

She nodded, not trusting her voice.

Daniel offered his arm, but Megan pretended not to notice and hurried back along the frosty path towards the road. The link she thought she'd formed with Daniel must have been all in her mind. Now she felt alone again, separate. Lonely.

Suddenly, she wanted nothing more than to be at home in the world she knew, away from the bustle of London and these people.

"I'm sorry, Megan," Daniel said as they reached the hotel doors. She shrugged out of his jacket and tossed it at him.

"There's nothing to be sorry about. I appreciate your company tonight."

"Megan."

Daniel's soft entreaty halted her rush through the door and she turned.

He raked back his hair with his fingers, a pained look in his eyes. They stared at each other for long moments, then she tore her gaze away and rushed into the warm hotel.

He was out of her league. How could she ever have thought he would be interested in her?

Chapter Three

Daniel dumped his bags and snowboard case beside a bench outside the tiny Scottish train station and sat down. The cold stung his face and nipped at his fingers while he waited for Duncan to pick him up. The place was silent, hardly a soul about. A bird of prey soared overhead and the wind whistled through a stand of pines nearby.

He'd felt terrible all week, and he didn't feel much better now. The last thing he'd wanted to do on New Year's Eve was hurt Megan, yet he had. But surely it was best to quash any romantic notions she had, rather than let her hope there could be something between them?

Even if he hadn't decided to give the army his undivided attention for another six months, it would be career suicide to mess with his commanding officer's sister. He would not screw up his chance at a new life for a romantic relationship that might be over in a few months. This time he'd put his long-term future before short-term pleasure.

A noisy diesel engine snagged his attention. He stared at the narrow road, waiting for the vehicle to appear. A muddy Land Rover pickup full of dents crested the ridge and lurched down the hill. He smiled to himself. One wouldn't see anything like that in

London. The vehicle was probably older than him.

The vehicle came to a halt and Duncan climbed out, wearing army uniform. Daniel gaped for a moment before he remembered to hide his astonishment.

Duncan held out his hand. Daniel jumped to his feet and shook it. "Hello, sir."

"Call me Duncan. We don't stand on ceremony here." He grabbed one of Daniel's bags and dumped it on the bed of the old pickup. Daniel dropped the other beside it and laid his snowboard over the top.

"Good journey?" Duncan inquired.

"A long journey. I could fly to New York in the time it took me to reach here."

Daniel climbed in beside Duncan, trying to get comfortable on the cracked vinyl bench seat. He reached for the seat belt, but there wasn't one. Duncan noticed.

"Most of the journeys this old girl makes are on private estate roads. She's probably not legal on normal roads."

Duncan pressed his foot on the clutch and slammed the gearshift into place with an eye-watering crunch, then the vehicle lurched forward.

"Clutch is a bit sticky," Duncan said as Daniel grabbed the door and what passed for a dashboard.

"How far is it to your place?"

"Only a few miles. We'll take the scenic route."

"Sounds great," Daniel said, wanting nothing more than to arrive at the destination so he could get out of this death trap.

At the bottom of a hill, Duncan swerved onto a rustic road and they bumped along the stones. For the umpteenth time, Daniel held on to the door to stay in his seat.

Mist hung beneath the close-packed trees on either side, an eerie half light turning the countryside mysterious as dusk fell.

"Sorry about the road surface," Duncan said, slamming the Land Rover down into a lower gear with a nasty grating sound. Daniel was starting to understand why the Scotsman used an old vehicle. Anything modern would be ruined in no time. If Daniel tried to bring his sports car this way, he'd probably have a broken axle by now.

They crested a steep hill, the engine whining. Duncan brought the vehicle to a stop and leaned on the steering wheel, staring out the windshield. "There you are, that's home. Kindrogan Castle."

A valley lay before them, a river meandering along the middle, white-water rapids visible in places. At the head of the valley, a gray stone castle sat by a loch, lawns running down to the water. Snowy mountain peaks framed the scene.

Daniel sucked in a breath and blew it out. He'd stayed in some amazing places over the years, but nothing this spectacular. He tried to imagine Megan standing in that scene, on the lawn by the lake, and found he could. Megan belonged here among this natural grandeur in a way no other woman of his acquaintance would.

This last week he'd thought of her often, remembered the soft sound of her melodic accent, the way she angled her head as she listened, how she lowered her lashes to hide her eyes when he caught her staring at him.

There was something old-fashioned and noble about her, as if she had stepped out of an historical novel. She didn't belong in the same world he lived in. Sure, he had mixed with the rich and famous in fashionable hot spots around the world, but that existence seemed so superficial and fleeting compared to this place.

"Spectacular, isn't it?" Duncan prompted.

"Amazing. How old is the castle?"

"There's been Mackenzies living here since the

fourteenth century. They were declared rebels in 1584. Then in the 1700s, they were ardent Jacobites. The family has a turbulent history."

Daniel's gaze strayed past the castle to the snowy peaks. The clear, crisp air brought back memories of racing over fresh powder, his heart pounding. He couldn't wait to get out on his snowboard.

"Do you ski?" he asked Duncan.

"As soon as I learned to walk. We all can. Meg's the best. She had a shot at being on the Olympic team a few years ago."

"No kidding." There was a lot more to Megan than Daniel had thought. "Does she snowboard?"

"No. Perhaps you can teach her." Duncan glanced at him, his eyebrows raised.

"Maybe." He'd have to be careful not to spend too much time alone with her. That woman would get under his skin if he didn't watch out. In fact, she already had. Perhaps staying with the Mackenzies had been a bad idea. "Are you sure you don't mind putting me up?"

"Heck, no. Megan and I rattle around in that huge place on our own. Blair's usually posted overseas and our younger brother, Hew, lives in one of the estate cottages."

"What about Brigadier Mackenzie, or does he prefer to be called Sir Robert?"

"Dad spends most of his time in London these days and my mother lives in Barbados. She and Dad are only still married because they never see each other."

"Yeah, my parents have just split up. Marriages don't seem to last."

"Tell me about it." Duncan slammed the vehicle into gear with feeling and it bumped and jolted down the hill. They followed the track along the river and rounded the loch, halting outside the front of the castle.

Daniel wiped his damp palms on his thighs. His gaze

went to the door, but there was no sign of Megan. His pulse raced at the thought of meeting her again. Crazy, he didn't get nervous about seeing women, or he never had before.

He climbed out and stretched the kinks in his neck and back, eyeing the turrets and old stone walls coated in lichen. Staying here was going to be an interesting experience.

Duncan passed across his bags and grabbed his laptop from the vehicle.

A cold wind whistled down the valley, rippling the water on the loch. Daniel drew in a deep breath of air that smelled of pine trees and heather. It was so quiet here, the silence almost a living presence.

Two West Highland white terriers scampered around the side of the castle and dashed towards Duncan, their tails wagging like mad.

"Have you been good boys?" Duncan crouched to pat them and they wiggled around him, nuzzling his hands.

"You like animals?" he asked Daniel.

"I grew up with dogs."

"That's good. Meet Bruce and Torrie."

Daniel bent and petted the excited Westies, smiling at their antics as they vied for his attention.

"Better go and tell Meg we've arrived." Duncan headed for the castle, held open the heavy oak door, and stood aside for Daniel to pass into the high-ceilinged, wood-paneled entrance hall.

Daniel cocked his head and took in the ancient tapestries, shields, and weapons hanging on the walls. This really was like stepping back into the past.

A child's laughter caught his attention. A small boy scampered through a door, naked from the waist down.

With a gurgling laugh he headed for Duncan, who put down his bag and scooped the child into his arms. "How are you, Gus, laddie?"

"Fergus Mackenzie, you come back here and sit on your potty." Megan's voice came from close by, then she hurried through the door after the boy with a packet of wet wipes in her hand.

At the sight of them she halted, eyes wide, like a deer caught in headlights.

All week, Daniel had told himself he was imagining how he felt about Megan. It had been the glamour of the occasion and the fact it was his first time at the RAMC ball that made him see her through rose-colored spectacles.

But even though she looked less than elegant, wearing jeans and a sweatshirt, with her hair in a messy ponytail, his heart gave that same strange bump.

How inconvenient that just when he'd given up women, he found one he really liked.

Pleasure burned through Megan at the sight of Daniel's warm smile and blue eyes. During the last week, she'd tried to kid herself she didn't care about him. Now she had to admit the truth—he lit a fire inside her like no man she'd ever met.

"You're early," Megan blurted. What a fright she must look. She tugged to straighten her ponytail, pulled askew by small, sticky fingers, and resisted the temptation to glance at her front, certain those same sticky fingers had left their mark on her sweatshirt.

She'd thought she had an hour to tidy up, fix her hair and makeup, and change clothes before they arrived.

Pasting on a grin she stepped forward, hand extended, trying to recover her composure. "Welcome to Kindrogan Castle, Daniel. It's lovely to see you again."

"Hello, Megan. You have an amazing home here." He gripped her fingers and drew her close, pressing a kiss to her cheek.

Time slowed as she touched her lips to the roughness of his jaw and inhaled the smell of his skin. The days collapsed back a week to the New Year's Ball—to the heaven of dancing in his arms. With a conscious effort she retreated, putting some distance between them, stowing away this new precious experience of him to enjoy in private.

"Come through to the kitchen. I'll make you both a cup of tea." She gave Daniel a glance she hoped appeared casual. "I'm sure you could do with one after your journey. I know the plane and train up from London can be rather tiresome."

As she walked through the gloomy hall to the kitchen, her back tingled, hyperaware of Daniel behind her.

"Sit down and make yourself at home."

She put the kettle on the range and set the biscuit tin in front of him. "There's home-baked Scottish shortbread if you'd like some."

He lifted the lid and his lips quirked in a smile as he took a piece. Her heart danced with pleasure as he bit into the crumbly shortbread with a groan of appreciation. She had made them especially for him, but she would never tell.

Megan lifted her mischievous nephew from Duncan's arms. "Now, you wee rascal, back to the cloakroom with you."

After carrying Fergus to the small room off the hall, she sat him on his blue potty and stood over him while he finished. Then she pulled on his trainer pants and washed her hands before taking him back to the kitchen.

The kettle whistled and she passed Fergus to Duncan, then poured hot water into the teapot and covered it with a tartan tea cozy that had belonged to her grandmother. She set the pot on the table with the cups, milk jug, and sugar bowl.

When she sat down, Fergus reached for her. She took him back into her arms, cuddling the darling little boy close while he squirmed, reaching to tangle his fingers in her hair.

"Meg, Meg, Meg," he chanted, pulling her ponytail off-center again. She stopped resisting the inevitable and let him stroke her hair. Touching hair was his comforter when he was tired.

"I hope Daddy picks you up soon, precious, or you'll be asleep." Her younger brother, Hew, enjoyed spending time with his son and she hated for him to miss out. She rubbed noses with her nephew, then settled him in her arms while he sucked his thumb.

A glance up from beneath her lashes found Daniel watching her. Part of her would love to know what he was thinking, but if she did it would probably hurt her feelings. If he hadn't been attracted to her when she was all primped for the ball, he certainly wasn't going to be interested in her when she looked like this.

After she arrived home from London, she'd googled his name. Hundreds of images filled the computer screen of him with beautiful women at fashionable social events. Romantic relationships were obviously not a problem for him per se, so she had to assume the problem was her.

When he'd claimed her company at the ball, he was being pragmatic. After all, Duncan had asked him to escort her. Daniel had to bid on a woman or eat dinner with a vacant seat beside him. He'd simply tried to impress his new commanding officer by keeping the wallflower sister happy.

During the next six weeks while he stayed, she would have to keep her feelings hidden, but she'd rather spend time with him as friends than not at all.

Her youngest brother, Hew, arrived and took his sleepy son home. Much as Megan loved babysitting Fergus, she was not sorry when Hew collected him.

Their housekeeper, Mrs. Stewart, was away caring for her sick sister, leaving Megan to hold the fort. She was so busy keeping house, babysitting Fergus, and working, she hardly had time to sleep at the moment.

Megan checked the venison casserole in the oven and sipped her tea between peeling potatoes. She let the pleasant timbre of Daniel's voice wash over her as he and Duncan discussed work at the army institute. Once the potatoes were in the pot to boil, she turned back to the men.

"Daniel, shall I show you to your room so you can clean up before dinner?"

"Yes. That'll be great. Thanks."

With quick strides, Megan headed to the foot of the stairs and slung the strap of Daniel's snowboard case over her shoulder, leaving him to carry his other two bags. She led him up the wide stairs, trying to see the place through the eyes of a stranger.

Discolored old family portraits lined the walls and the ancient wooden paneling was carved with Celtic symbols from antiquity.

"That's the Mackenzie coat of arms, isn't it?" Daniel pointed at a shield above the front door.

"That's right. How did you know?"

"You showed me your brooch last weekend."

Her heart skipped then jigged at the thought he had remembered such a thing. She silently reprimanded herself for being silly. It would be so easy to fall into the trap of reading hidden meaning into things Daniel said and did. That way lay heartbreak.

Turning onto the landing that overlooked the entrance hall, she trod along the creaky floorboards to the end bedroom. She had given him a large room with views from two sides: over Loch Kinder, and towards the mountains.

She opened the door and led him in, placing his snowboard case across the wooden arms of a chair. "I hope you like the room."

"Fantastic." He dropped his bags and glanced around, his gaze pausing on the four-poster bed.

Megan's eyes strayed to the bed she had made up for him with the loving care no normal guest received. Her cheeks heated, remembering some of her thoughts as she'd smoothed the sheets.

He wandered across to check the view of the snowy peaks through the window. "Wow. I can't wait to get out there on my snowboard."

"Snow is one thing we have plenty of up here at this time of year."

"Perhaps you can show me the best slopes sometime? I'll let you try out my snowboard."

"I prefer skis." The truth was she had never used a snowboard. Her father thought that snowboarding was for tearaways. A stupid prejudice, really, since snowboarding was an Olympic sport. She shrugged. "Maybe I'll give snowboarding a try. Are you free next weekend?"

Daniel grinned, his blue eyes glinting with happiness that she felt right down to her toes. "Absolutely. It's a date!"

Chapter Four

The sound of noisy dogs woke Daniel. He lay staring up at the red fabric canopy of the old four-poster bed, listening to the commotion outside his window. Voices mingled with the excited barking. He was certain he heard Megan.

He climbed out of bed, goose bumps streaking over his bare chest in the chill. Rubbing his arms, he padded barefoot across the wooden floorboards to the window. A gap between the curtains gave him a view of the yard below.

Five dogs frolicked: Duncan's two Westies, a couple of cairn terriers, and a Jack Russell. Young Fergus dashed around with the dogs while the boy's father stood chatting with a grizzled old guy and a policeman who leaned back against a four-wheel drive police vehicle.

To start with, Daniel couldn't see Megan, although he was certain he'd heard her. Then she strode into view carrying a tray of steaming mugs that she passed out to the men. They chatted and laughed, Megan cheerful and relaxed.

This morning she wore a knee-length tartan skirt and black leather boots, her hair pinned up with a shiny clip. She waved her expressive hands while she talked, frequently laughing, angling her head to listen

31

in a way somehow both cute and elegant. Daniel leaned forward and pressed his nose to the glass. Megan Mackenzie was a beautiful, unique woman.

It looked as though the policeman thought so too. The man watched her, especially when she wasn't looking.

Daniel shifted, irritated, wishing he could go down there and tell the guy to leave her alone.

A sigh of relief whispered between Daniel's lips when the policeman opened his car door. "That's right, buddy, off you go."

Megan carried the mugs away on the tray and returned a few moments later wearing a jacket, her handbag over her arm. She climbed in the passenger seat of the police cruiser.

"No way. You're kidding me." Daniel slapped a palm against the window frame in frustration as the vehicle pulled off. He dashed across his room to the other window to see the police car take the road around the loch.

Where was she going with the guy?

Daniel raked back his hair and blew out a breath. "It doesn't matter. She's out of bounds."

Yeah, right. He needed to keep telling himself because it wasn't sinking in.

He was so deep in thought, a knock on his bedroom door made him jump. Striding across the room, he wrenched the door open, still irritated.

Duncan stood there already dressed in uniform.

"Huh?" Daniel had been so busy watching Megan he hadn't thought to check the time. "Sorry, am I late?" A fine start to his first day working at the army institute.

"Don't worry. I'm not planning to leave for another hour. I have a few things to sort out here. Megan's left your breakfast in the warming oven, but first I need to show you how the bathroom works."

Still distracted by what he'd seen, Daniel slung his

towel around his neck, grabbed his wash bag, and followed Duncan along the corridor.

"I saw a policeman outside."

"That'd be Lyall. He's police liaison for the Kindrogan Mountain Rescue Team. He's around here a lot."

"Megan got in his car." A hint of annoyance crept into Daniel voice.

Duncan cast him a curious look, a slight smile on his lips. "He gives her a lift into work sometimes. Does it bother you?"

Clenching his teeth, Daniel shook his head and pushed aside the battery of questions he wanted to ask. He needed to let this go and concentrate on why he was here.

Duncan opened the bathroom door. An old claw-foot tub sat near the wall, a shower coming off the faucet. An ancient sink stood under the window. The room reminded him of his days at boarding school.

"Gosh, it's cold in here." Duncan thumped the cast iron radiator that looked like it belonged in a museum. He twisted the taps on the bath. The pipes knocked, but no water appeared.

"Damn plumbing is so unreliable. We probably need the whole system upgraded."

Daniel agreed wholeheartedly, yet refrained from commenting.

"I was worried this might happen. You'll have to use Meg's bathroom. She won't mind."

Duncan led Daniel back past his room to the other end of the corridor and down some steps. Two doors faced each other in this more modern part of the castle. "That's Meg's bedroom," Duncan said with a gesture, "and this is her bathroom."

He pushed open the door and a blissful cloud of fragrant, steamy heat enveloped Daniel.

"The shower definitely works in here," Duncan said.

"I'll see you downstairs in a minute."

The welcome warmth seeped into Daniel's chilled body as he glanced around. With a sink, bath, and shower that had been fitted sometime in living memory, this was a lot more comfortable.

A bathmat draped over the side of the bath, a net bag of child's bath toys hung over the faucet. Megan's toiletries and towels were all neatly arranged. She must be a tidy person. He loved discovering such details like puzzle pieces he could fit together to learn who she was.

A small makeup bag sat on the shelf. He touched his fingertips to the silky fabric, then picked up a perfume bottle and sniffed. With almost guilty pleasure, he inhaled the sweet fragrance of Megan.

After the ball, his jacket had smelled of her perfume. Every time he opened his wardrobe, he caught a whiff. This last week he had found numerous excuses to look inside his wardrobe, just so he could breathe in Megan's fragrance.

He draped his towel over the radiator, stripped off his pajama pants, and stepped into the shower. The smell of her toiletries lingered. He stood beneath the hot spray, loath to soap himself with his own shower gel and wipe out her delicate fragrance.

This was crazy. He should be focusing on his new posting at the army institute, but he just wanted the week to be over so he could go skiing with Megan. He had been here for less than a day and the woman was already taking over his psyche.

The crisp snow crunched beneath Megan's boots as she walked around the Land Rover to take her skis off the back of the vehicle.

Daniel joined her to grab his snowboard case. "This is a fantastic spot. I can't wait to get going." Flashing a grin, he unclipped the molded plastic and pulled the snowboard out.

He stowed the case back in the vehicle and wandered away, fitting his goggles over his hat and zipping up his jacket.

Angus Stewart, who had worked for Megan's father on Kindrogan Estate since he was sixteen, handed over her ski poles before slamming the back of the Land Rover closed.

"You go careful now, lass. Call me if you get into trouble." He patted the pocket of his Barbour jacket that contained his phone.

"We'll be fine, Angus. You know me. I'm always careful."

The old man's gaze flicked to Daniel, then back. He leaned closer and lowered his voice. "Just make sure you dinnae let that one lead you astray."

Megan suppressed a smile as she glanced at Daniel in his frameless mirror goggles and brightly colored designer ski wear that screamed tourist. Of course, the snowboard alone was enough to put Angus's back up.

"Text me if the weather forecast changes," she told him. "If conditions stay like this, meet us at the bottom in three hours."

"Will do, lass." Angus touched his cap. With a last suspicious glance at Daniel, he limped back to the driver's door and climbed in. He backed the vehicle up and crunched through the snow down the track to Kindrogan.

Megan snapped her boots into the bindings on her skis and skied over to Daniel. He stood with his arms akimbo, staring out across the countryside.

"This is awe-inspiring. I can see why you like it here. Living in London, one tends to forget we have places like this in the UK."

Megan drew in a breath of clean mountain air, the cold bite in her lungs giving her a thrill. Her heart thumped, blood surging, excitement bubbling at the prospect of a fast downhill run.

Snowy peaks stretched into the distance as far as the eye could see. She pointed and named a few of the well-known mountains. "You can see some of the runs at Glenshee from here."

Daniel nodded. "Glad we're not there with the crowd. I love off-piste boarding. The farther out in the backwoods, the better."

Pristine, unbroken snow lay before them with a fine powder coat. It was a perfect day for skiing, the sky slightly overcast with patches of blue, and no wind.

"Okay, you ready?" She glanced at Daniel. She had to discipline herself not to gaze at him too much. He was so gorgeous, she could happily stare at him all day. He'd wiped some white sun block over his lips. It shouldn't be sexy, but it was.

He strapped his back boot into the binding on his snowboard and skated forward to the lip of the plateau and stared down the fall line while he buckled in his front foot. She had no doubt he'd give her a run for her money if they raced, but that wasn't safe off-piste.

"I know the country, so I'll lead."

He gave her a teasing look, his eyes twinkling with mischief. "You afraid I'll beat you if we race?"

"No. I'm afraid you'll smack into a rock or go over the edge of a precipice."

"Don't worry. I have no intention of smacking anything. I'll follow wherever you lead, sweetheart." The teasing note in his voice brought a flush to her cheeks. She might believe he was flirting with her if she didn't know better.

She pulled down her goggles and Daniel did the same. Then she poled forward and dropped over the lip, quickly picking up speed down the slope. Cold air whipped her face, stealing her breath until she acclimatized. She flew through the air, rocks and trees a blur as she passed, a heady rush of excitement mixed with a hint of danger.

This was when she felt truly alive, in the countryside she loved, the cold air in her face, the snow singing beneath her as she zigzagged down the hill, carving out a path with her skis. Sharing this experience with Daniel was wonderful. From the corner of her eye she saw him streaking along beside her, jumping over bumps, as good on his board as she was on her skis.

She rolled her knees into a sweeping turn and pulled up. Daniel slewed around, spraying her with snow that rattled off her jacket and trousers as he came to a dramatic halt at her side.

Such a show-off!

"Looking good, Meg." Daniel raised his eyebrows and nodded with approval. "You're right at home on those skis."

She blushed under his praise. Wintry sun broke through the clouds, beaming down on them. Everything seemed brighter, the pines greener, the snow whiter, the smell of the air cleaner as if being with Daniel sharpened her senses.

"You're not too shabby yourself."

He gave a theatrical bow and she laughed.

"I stopped to show you the view." Megan pointed at the vista of Kindrogan Castle below, the river a gleaming ribbon of silver meandering along the valley between rolling hills to the small village of Kinder Vale in the distance.

"Wow! That's so cool." Daniel pulled his phone from his pocket and snapped some photos. "I must send a picture to my brother."

They skied on, slaloming between stands of trees and rocky outcrops. Daniel jumped off a small drop, whooping with excitement as he flew through the air to land in a burst of snow. The next time they reached a plateau Daniel shot past her, angling the side of his board into the snow, to circle to a halt. She pulled up as well.

"Why've we stopped?" she asked.

"This is the perfect place for your snowboarding lesson."

"Oh." Megan wasn't sure she wanted to fall over in front of him.

He unfastened his bindings and Megan did the same, upending her skis in the snow so they didn't slide away.

He beckoned her closer, a mischievous smile on his lips. "Now, Miss Mackenzie, tell me what you know about snowboarding?"

"Nothing, really."

"Ah, a snowboarding virgin. My favorite kind."

Megan's embarrassed laugh burst across the hushed mountainside.

He gave her some basic instruction and crouched to strap her boots into the bindings. "The stance won't be quite right for you as you're shorter than me, but it's okay for a start."

Balance wasn't a problem for her, but it was so weird having both feet fixed to one thing. The principle of changing direction was the same as for skis, carving the edge of the board in the snow, but she had to tilt her body differently to achieve that. She glided forward, angled her hips for a turn, and landed on her backside in the snow.

"I know why men like snowboards. They're the motorbikes of the snow sports world," she said with a hint of sarcasm in her tone.

Daniel laughed. "Good analogy." He gave her his arm and helped her back on her feet.

He placed a hand on either side of her waist to steady her. "Bend your knees and angle your hips, like this," he said, demonstrating the movement. Megan attempted to copy him and he nodded.

"Okay, move off and try again."

Megan angled across the gentle slope, shifting her weight to tilt the board.

"Lean left," Daniel shouted. Megan tried, but she felt herself falling, then Daniel's arm swept under her back, breaking her fall. Laughing, they landed in a heap together in the soft snow. Pulse racing, Megan grabbed a breath as tiny cold ice crystals stung her hot cheeks.

"Don't you know your left from your right?" Daniel said. "You leaned the wrong way."

Daniel was so close, lying in the snow at her side. He boosted himself on an elbow and stared down at her. Her normally sharp brain seemed to be full of cotton wool. It was highly possible she had muddled up left and right. She couldn't seem to think with him this close.

Her chest tightened with longing as she stared into his laughing blue eyes. She hadn't been able to stop thinking about him since the New Year's ball. Whenever she had a quiet moment, thoughts of Daniel filled her mind. Every night he swept into her dreams and kissed her senseless.

He leaned in to wipe a spot of snow from her cheek with the thumb of his glove. His smile fell away and tiny lines appeared between his eyebrows, a sudden intensity in his eyes. "Megan. What I said the other night, after the ball..."

He pulled off his glove and cupped his warm fingers around her cheek. Were her dreams about to come true? Was he going to kiss her? As he moved closer, her eyelids drifted closed. Time slowed; the silence deepened.

Wind hummed among the pine needles. Megan held her breath, anticipating the blissful moment when Daniel's lips touched hers. Then the strident chime of her phone cut through the silence.

Snatching a breath, Daniel pulled back. He stood and busied himself brushing the snow from his clothes.

With a burst of irritation, Megan plucked apart Velcro and snatched the phone from her pocket.

"Great! I got you." It was Lyall's voice. Blast him for interrupting.

"What is it?" she snapped.

"A call came in to mountain rescue from a teenager who was climbing with his father and brother. The father's had a fall."

His words jolted Megan out of her romantic haze and back to reality. Her mountain rescue work took priority over everything. This was someone's life at stake.

"We'll be at the pickup point at the bottom of Kinder Fall in fifteen minutes. Can your dad fetch us then?"

"No problem. I'll tell him now."

Megan unbuckled the snowboard bindings and stood, dusting herself off. "We need to go straight down. I have to work." Romantic kisses would have to wait for another time.

Chapter Five

Angus hit the accelerator. They bounced over rocks and into potholes like they were on a fairground ride. Daniel didn't mind being shaken around in the front of the ancient Land Rover with Megan squashed up beside him. In a small way it made up for missing out on the kiss he'd looked forward to.

Megan braced herself against Daniel's side so she didn't end up in his lap. That would not have been a problem as far as he was concerned. Although from the scowl on old Angus's face, he might not have approved.

The bumpy journey ended too soon, the irascible Angus stopping the Land Rover outside the headquarters of the Kindrogan Mountain Rescue Team. The building was about half a mile from Kindrogan Castle, housed in a converted farm building.

Angus glared from beneath his bushy gray eyebrows as Daniel fumbled with the door handle and climbed out. He wasn't sure what he'd done to upset the old guy, but he obviously didn't like him.

A new Land Rover was parked nearby with Kindrogan Mountain Rescue and the Scottish mountain rescue logo on the side.

"All right if I tag along?" Daniel asked as Megan jumped out.

"You want to come on the rescue?"

He nodded. He wanted to spend as much time with her as possible. "I might be able to help."

She frowned in thought. "Don't see why not. You can handle yourself in the snow and you do have avalanche training. Come on, let's go inside and see who's turned up. If there's a spare place on the team, you can come."

Megan shoved open the door to a small office full of men. The conversation quieted when they entered and the group parted to let her through.

Lyall stood by the far wall, pointing at a map. "Good, you're here," he said. Megan went to stand at his side.

Daniel stepped in beside Megan's younger brother, Hew, and nodded in greeting. Hew was a younger, leaner version of Duncan, and a man of few words. Daniel had never gotten more than a nod or brief greeting from him.

Leaning a shoulder against the back wall, Daniel crossed his arms, happy to keep a low profile, watch, and learn.

"What have we got?" Megan asked.

"A father and his two teenage sons were climbing here." Lyall tapped the map with his finger. "The father fell, about fifty feet by the sound of it. Apparently he blacked out for a while but he's conscious now. The two boys climbed down to reach him."

"Are the kids injured?"

"Not that we know of. The helicopter from RAF Lossiemouth has been scrambled. It'll pick us up at Kinder Flat in twenty minutes."

"I reckon they should drop us at Glen Duff. We can hike in from there," one of the older guys said.

There was a general mumble of agreement in the room.

"Before we go, let me introduce Dan." Megan extended a hand in his direction. Everyone looked around. "He'll be coming with us."

"We don't have time for passengers," Lyall snapped.

"He's no passenger. He's an army doctor working with Duncan at the institute. He's had avalanche training."

Lyall's lips flattened in obvious annoyance. He had the sort of dark good looks women went for. Daniel wouldn't be surprised if Megan returned the man's interest, although she hadn't shown any indication of that so far.

"We're two men short, so Dan will be useful," one of the team said. Most of the others added their agreement.

A guy near Daniel slapped him on the back. "Welcome aboard, mate."

Megan pulled off her fleece hat and retied her ponytail, scraping her silky red hair back in her hands before slipping the stretchy band on again. Daniel watched Lyall checking her out and clenched his teeth. He didn't remember feeling this possessive of a woman before, especially one he wasn't even dating.

"Okay. Let's pack the gear and go," Lyall said.

They trooped out of the room and grabbed bags, ropes, climbing gear, a stretcher, and other stuff from a storeroom. Hew passed Daniel a couple of bags. He carried them out and tossed them on the rack on top of the Land Rover as the others did. Then he clambered in the back of the vehicle, squashed in with the rest of the team.

Megan climbed in the front with Lyall, casting Daniel a smile over her shoulder as they pulled away. Five minutes later, they stopped at a flat cement area about a mile from the castle. The sound of a helicopter approaching caught Daniel's attention as they dragged the packs and equipment off the top of the vehicle.

A yellow RAF Sea King touched down and they all ran towards it, tossed the gear in the open door, then vaulted up inside.

"Daniel, over here." Megan called him to sit beside

her near a window. Once they had taken off, she gripped his sleeve to attract his attention. "Check out the view," she shouted above the drone of the engine, pointing at the window.

The helicopter flew over Kindrogan Castle, giving a fantastic outlook down the Kinder Valley.

Daniel leaned close to her ear, breathing in a taste of her fragrance before he spoke. "ETA?"

"Fifteen minutes," Megan shouted. "We're lucky the weather's good, otherwise the helicopter wouldn't get into Glen Duff. We'd have to be dropped farther away and walk in. That makes a rescue take much longer. Today we should be in and out quickly."

In the week Daniel had been here, he'd discovered if you took too long to blink the weather changed. It was so unpredictable. He wouldn't want to be injured up in the mountains.

The scenery slid by the window. Banter flew around the group as they ribbed each other and traded insults, just like any group of men preparing to face a challenging situation. Megan remained silent, her gaze fixed in the distance. Her coping strategy was different.

Daniel gripped her hand where it lay in her lap and squeezed. "Okay?" he mouthed.

She smiled at him and his heart did the flip and bump thing it only ever did when she was around. The Sea King climbed steadily into the mountains on the other side of Glenshee, the skiers tiny colored dots against the white snow.

Lyall wore a headset to communicate with the pilot. "They've spotted three people. We're about to land." At his words, the banter ceased. Everyone zipped up their jackets, pulled on their hats and gloves, and prepared themselves.

The helicopter touched down. As the door was opened, they all grabbed packs and equipment. Hew took one end of the stretcher and Daniel grabbed the other.

A stiff, freezing wind whipped into Daniel's face as he climbed out, stealing his breath. In this temperature it wouldn't take long to get into trouble, even though the weather looked fine. They traipsed through thick snow, sometimes slipping on icy rocks, sometimes sinking up to their thighs in snow-filled dips. A few hundred yards away at the base of a cliff, two people waited in bright gear beside what must be the injured man.

Megan strode on ahead. Daniel passed off the stretcher to someone else and hurried to catch up with her in case she needed him.

She clambered up the rocks to the casualty, put down her medical pack, and dropped to her knees. Daniel moved to the other side of the man. He was bleeding from the mouth and nose, his face covered in multiple lacerations and contusions. After such a fall, the odds were he had sustained multiple fractures, and a possible head injury as well.

"Hell," Daniel whispered under his breath. The poor guy was a mess. The kids looked terrified, their faces white masks of distress. The older boy was holding it together, the younger not doing so well. Tears silently poured down his cheeks.

"I'm Dr. Mackenzie." Megan addressed the older boy. "What's your dad's name?"

"Marcus Smyth. Is he going to be all right?"

She didn't answer, her attention fixed on the casualty. "Marcus, can you hear me?"

She pressed her fingers to the carotid pulse in his neck.

The man's eyes fluttered open.

"Good," she whispered, her gaze skipping up to Daniel. "Thready pulse and breathing is shallow. Let's get him some oxygen." The mask was fitted over his face. Megan slid the man's hood off and quickly

45

examined his head.

She met Daniel's gaze, her lips pressed tight. "I can't do much for him here. We need to get him to the hospital as quickly as possible. I need help with the back brace." In a move they obviously practiced, her brother Hew and another man helped slide the support beneath Marcus Smyth and strap it on to stabilize his spine in case of injury.

"How far did your dad fall?" Daniel asked the boys.

"From up there." The older boy pointed at the mountain. Ropes still dangled from the rock face about fifty feet above.

"Okay. Let's get him on the stretcher," Megan said.

Daniel stepped out of the way as the team moved in, working together in a well-practiced routine to load the man and cover him in thermal wraps to keep him warm.

The younger boy sobbed. Daniel crouched on the rocks in front of him so he could see his face. "What's your name?"

"Kieran."

"Your dad will be in the hospital soon. The doctors there will do all they can to make him better."

"It was my fault," the boy whispered.

"I'm sure your dad doesn't blame you."

"One of my gloves blew away and Dad gave me his. He couldn't hold on 'cause his hand got cold."

Daniel glanced at the man but his hands were now covered. He turned his attention back to the boy. "How long did you go without a glove, Kieran?" It wouldn't take long for this freezing wind to do damage to unprotected fingers.

"I don't remember."

"Show me the hand that lost the glove, son." It was obvious which one it must be. The glove on his left hand was far too big. Daniel helped him ease it off, his breath stalling at the blotchy white skin. He had definitely suffered tissue damage; the question was how badly.

He gently slid the glove back in place. There was nothing he could do for Kieran here. "Does your hand hurt?"

The boy nodded, tears rolling down his cheeks.

Daniel grabbed a sling out of Megan's medical kit and strapped the boy's arm against his body to protect the hand. With luck, the damage was only mild frostbite and the tissue would recover. It would take a few weeks to be sure. If it turned out to be serious, Daniel would offer to operate.

The skin, subcutaneous tissues, and blood supply were things he knew a lot about from his work as a cosmetic surgeon, which was why his expertise meshed so well with thermal medicine. If this child was likely to lose fingers, he needed a surgeon who could preserve the function of the hand as much as possible.

Daniel was not one for false modesty. He was an excellent plastic surgeon, certainly as good as his brother. They needed to take this child to the army institute where Daniel could look after him.

Staring at Megan across the table as she licked ice cream off her spoon, Daniel really wished the phone hadn't interrupted them earlier when they were on the ski slope.

He wanted to kiss her very much. The reasons he'd had for holding back now seemed unimportant. Fighting the attraction was tying him in knots rather than helping him concentrate on work.

And as for Megan being his commanding officer's sister, that could turn out to be a good thing. She knew army doctors had to go where they were posted. She wouldn't expect him to always be around.

"You obviously enjoyed that dessert," he said with a grin.

She set aside her bowl with a satisfied smile. "Fancy a mug of cocoa spiked with a wee dram of whiskey? We can finish off the evening in front of the fire."

"Sounds like heaven." After the day they'd had, Daniel couldn't think of anything he'd rather do than curl up in front of the fire with Megan.

He was fit, but snowboarding followed by a stint with the mountain rescue team had taken its toll. He was more than ready to relax.

Megan heated milk and Daniel spooned cocoa powder and sugar into two mugs. After she poured out the milk, he slopped in a generous splash of Scottish double malt. His father would consider it sacrilege to waste a fine whiskey this way. The thought made Daniel smile. Crazy as it seemed, he missed his overbearing father. When he returned from his upcoming cold weather training in Norway, he would go home for a visit.

"Angus lit the fire earlier. It should be nice and warm in the drawing room."

Daniel followed Megan along the corridor, the two Westies, Bruce and Torrie, trotting at his feet. Duncan had gone to Edinburgh for the weekend and the dogs seemed to have adopted Daniel as their surrogate master. They'd been curled on his bed when he arrived home.

Stepping into the drawing room was like stepping back in time. The electric wall lights were candle-shaped and cast a pale glow over the room. The huge roaring log fire was topped with a mantel lined with antiques and hunting trophies. Oil paintings of majestic Scottish scenes adorned the walls along with a couple of shields, some crossed spears, and a stag's head. Light from the fire flickered over the scene like something from a bygone era.

Bruce and Torrie went straight to the mat in front of the fire and claimed prime position, staring up at him with their black button eyes. He crouched to stroke them, waiting to see where Megan settled before choosing his own seat. She plopped down in an armchair to one side of the fire and curled her feet beneath her, wrapping her hands around her mug.

No cuddling up on the leather sofa then. Daniel took the armchair facing her. The dogs immediately came to lie at his feet. "I'm not sure what I've done to deserve such adoration." He laughed.

Without commenting, Megan stared up at him from beneath her lashes, a knowing smile on her face.

Out on the slopes when they'd been having fun together, it was much easier to get close to Megan. Being at Kindrogan with her was like stepping into a more genteel world. All his usual flirtatious small talk seemed frivolous or inappropriate. Normally if he was attracted to a woman, he knew how to behave. The people in his circle understood how the relationship game was played. For the first time in many years, he was unsure how to proceed.

"I'm tired," she said, letting her head rest on the chair back. "It's been a long day."

"I enjoyed the skiing this morning."

She smiled. "Me too. It's a shame we were interrupted."

"My thoughts exactly." He sipped his cocoa, enjoying the kick of the whiskey as it reached his stomach.

For a moment, he recalled lying in the snow with Megan, the anticipation of the kiss. Then his thoughts drifted on to the fallen climber, and to Kieran Smyth. His pleasure dimmed slightly. The poor kid had a tough time ahead of him.

"I'm worried about the Smyth boy. You know that after the hospital warmed up his hand, they just dressed it and sent him home with a few painkillers? The presenting symptoms might not look like much

49

now, but there's a strong risk of necrosis. The poor boy might end up losing some of his fingers. They should keep him in for observation and pain management."

"You're not in the ivory towers of private practice anymore. Welcome to the real world of budget cuts and bed shortages in the National Health Service." Megan heaved a resigned sigh.

She scooped back her silky hair and let it fall over her shoulders in a mesmerizing red-gold cascade that distracted Daniel from the conversation.

He cleared his throat and gathered his thoughts. "When I trained, I did the usual rotation in the National Health hospitals like you did."

"Well, you've forgotten the reality, then."

"I guess you're right." This was exactly why he'd wanted to get his feet back on the ground and really help people, rather than cater to the whims of the über wealthy.

"By the way, you did a great job noticing the lad was injured. I was so occupied with the father, I would have missed it."

Daniel shrugged. "You focused on the serious casualty. I'd have done the same if I were on my own."

As they were talking, it seemed like a good time to ask a question that had been bugging him. "By the way, what's the deal with you and Lyall? Are you dating or something?"

She burst out laughing, spitting drips of cocoa down her front. "Now look what you made me do." She pulled a tissue from her pocket and mopped herself.

When she'd finished, she leaned back with an amused sigh. "Lyall's like a brother to me. He's Angus's son. We grew up together. I can't wait to tell him you thought we were dating. He'll have a good laugh at that."

No, he won't, Daniel thought. The poor guy was obviously in love with Megan and she had no idea.

Daniel almost felt sorry for him.

Tapping his fingers on the arm of the chair, he watched her finish her cocoa and set the cup aside. He longed to kiss Megan, but first he wanted to romance her, to make her feel special. He wanted to make up for hurting her feelings after the New Year's ball.

An iPod docking station sat on a chest beside a stuffed fox. Setting his mug aside, Daniel pulled out his phone and selected a romantic track, one they could dance to. He rose, stepped over the dogs, and slotted his phone in place, pressing play.

The soulful strains of a slow song filled the air. He extended a hand towards Megan. "Will you dance with me, sweetheart?"

Her eyes widened in that deer-in-the-headlights look she did so well, appearing cute and vulnerable rather than startled. As she stared at him, he had a tense moment when he feared she might refuse. Then she rose to her feet and slid her slender fingers into his palm.

Megan let Daniel draw her into his arms, hanging on to her good sense by a thread. She would not let the pleasure of his embrace turn her into a senseless ninny like it had at the New Year's ball. Flirting obviously came to him as naturally as breathing, but he'd made it absolutely clear the first night they met that he didn't want a romantic relationship with her.

He was just passing the time and having a bit of fun. She was the only woman here, so if he wanted to flirt, it was with her or not at all.

He drew her closer, his hand sliding up to cradle the back of her head and ease it against his shoulder.

"Relax," he whispered.

She wanted to. Her heart had gone all warm and fuzzy, her muscles soft with desire, but her common sense retained a corner of her brain. Even as his hand stroked warm circles of sensation on her back, his words from New Year's Eve played through her mind.

He didn't want a relationship with her.

Yet he confused her. She was halfway in love with the charming man whose company she enjoyed, the kind man who'd taken Kieran Smyth under his wing. But the Daniel she knew didn't connect with what she'd found out about him on Google or what Olivia had said.

The spicy fragrance of Daniel's aftershave filled her nose, his stubble rough against her temple. Dreamy sensation whispered through her, wiping her mind of worries. Being in Daniel's arms was her fantasy. Why was she resisting? His embrace tightened and his lips pressed against her hair.

Daniel Fabian had stormed his way into her heart. Despite her best defenses, she could not resist him.

"I can't stop thinking about you," Daniel whispered.

Even though Megan knew he was just sweet-talking her, she melted inside.

"I love being with you, sweetheart." As he continued, her legs went all wobbly at the knees.

He stopped in front of the fire and put a finger beneath her chin, tilting her face up. Firelight danced over his golden hair, turned his beautiful face into a sculpture of light and shadow. Any doubts Megan had dissolved at the flash of desire in his blue eyes.

"Daniel." Her befuddled brain could manage nothing but his name, whispered in the reverential tone of a prayer. Her heart ached; she loved him so much. She had never felt like this before, never known it was possible to yearn so hard for a man to care for her.

Lowering his head, he brushed his lips across hers. Her breath caught, her heart stumbled, and she fell into the blissful sensation as he deepened the kiss.

After long moments, he pulled back and stroked a finger across her cheek, a smile on his face. "You're adorable."

Daniel Fabian was a master of sweet words that probably meant nothing. Even as she drowned in the pleasure, pain pulsed through her heart.

She hoped the old saying, "It's better to have loved and lost than never to have loved at all," was true. She had a nasty feeling she would soon find out.

Chapter Six

A young army nurse knocked on Daniel's consulting-room door and popped her head inside. "Kieran Smyth is here to see you, sir. Shall I show him in?"

"No. I'll come out."

Daniel rose, relieved to leave the report he was writing. He couldn't concentrate with thoughts of Megan constantly bugging him. He had barely seen her since their kiss two weeks ago. Most evenings she'd worked late and last weekend she'd disappeared off to a wedding with Lyall.

After the kiss, he'd expected them to grow closer and things to heat up. Instead she'd backed off, or that's the way it seemed.

He'd been certain she liked him. What had he done wrong?

He blew out a frustrated breath and pulled open his door. A short walk down a corridor took him to the waiting room. The clinic was small scale. Being so specialized, only a few civilian outpatients visited. Most of the cases he'd dealt with since he started three weeks ago had been joint forces personnel who were admitted directly onto the ward from active service.

The moment Mrs. Smyth's anxious face came into view, guilt filled Daniel. Here he was moping about his love life, or lack of it, when the poor Smyth family really did have things to worry about.

This was Kieran's third visit to the clinic for his injury to be monitored. "Hello, Kieran." Daniel smiled at the boy. His damaged hand was splinted, bandaged, and held immobile against his body in a sling. "Hello, Mrs. Smyth. How are things?"

The woman rose, her gaze brightening. "Hello, Dr. Fabian. Thank you so much for seeing Kieran again."

"You're welcome. I'm glad to help. I gather Mr. Smyth is making good progress."

Tears filled her eyes and she dropped her gaze. "So they say, but he'll be in the hospital for months. I don't know how we'll manage with him off work."

Daniel placed a hand on the woman's shoulder in silent support, not sure what to say. At least Mr. Smyth was expected to recover. Daniel hadn't seen much of Megan, but she had taken the time to keep him updated on that.

"Come through and we'll talk about Kieran." Daniel led the way to his room and ushered them inside. He tapped the back of the chair nearest his desk. "Sit here, Kieran. We'll take a look at your hand."

The boy and his mother sat down, both tense and pale. "How have you been since I last saw you?" Daniel asked the boy.

"My fingers tingle and burn sometimes, and they throb at night so I can't sleep."

Daniel nodded. The boy had been on a number of drugs: antibiotics, codeine, and a nonsteroidal anti-inflammatory. There was a limit to the type of pain relief Daniel could prescribe for home use. It might be time to admit Kieran to the ward and give him some morphine. That would make him more comfortable and help him sleep.

"The district nurse popped in to change the dressing as you requested," Mrs. Smyth said. "She said Kieran's fingers didn't look as bad as she expected."

55

"That sounds promising." Daniel gave them a smile, silently hoping the district nurse was right. He gently removed the boy's injured hand from the sling. "If you stretch out your arm, we'll take off the dressing and have a look, shall we?"

Daniel pulled on gloves, unwrapped the bandage, and set it aside in a plastic tray. He held the boy's left hand by the wrist and angled it to check the fingers. The skin had blistered and scabbed over in places, but the injury was proving to be less extensive than he'd feared. The nail on the little finger would fall off and the tip of that finger and the ring finger would need to be amputated, but the middle finger and index finger would not need surgery. The serious problem was going to be the thumb.

Supporting the damaged hand, he examined the thumb in more detail, carefully schooling his expression. "Okay, thank you." He rested the boy's hand back on the arm of his chair. "In a moment I'll ask a nurse to redress that for you."

"Will he need an operation?" Mrs. Smyth said.

"Yes. Let's talk about that. See where the ends of the two smallest fingers have discolored?" Mrs. Smyth nodded and Kieran stared at his hand. "That part of Kieran's fingers got frozen and will need to be removed. The good news is that once it heals, you'll quickly adapt and it shouldn't affect how you use your hand."

"What about my thumb?" Kieran tried to flex it and winced.

Daniel feared both the soft tissue and bone were necrotic. "Some of your thumb will have to be taken away, but I have lots of experience with reconstructive surgery. I'll make sure you can still use your thumb."

With five years of experience reshaping faces, often having to break bones to transform noses, cheekbones, brow bones, and jaws, repairing Kieran's thumb would be a cake walk. "It'll be a simple procedure. I'll replace the two small bones in the end of your thumb with a metal post and take a skin graft from your forearm to build you a new thumb."

"Will it hurt?" The boy's voice wobbled.

"You'll be asleep when I operate, but it will be sore for a while once it's done."

"And it'll work like his old thumb?" Mrs. Smyth asked.

"It won't feel quite the same, but with practice I'm sure Kieran will get used to it."

The boy nodded and gave Daniel a weak smile. Daniel returned it with feeling. He was a brave kid. Daniel would do his best to repair his thumb.

Megan added some sliced haggis to the pan beside the sizzling sausages and strips of bacon. Lyall stood a few feet away, his hip propped against the kitchen counter, cradling his coffee cup in his hands.

They were a sorry pair. Saturday morning and they were hanging out together because neither of them had significant others. Lyall was a good-looking man. He dated tourists sometimes, but his problem was the same as Meg's—nobody stuck around for long up here in the middle of nowhere. They all scurried back to the bright lights of the cities.

"Any plans for today?" Lyall asked.

Megan glanced over her shoulder to where Fergus sat in his high chair, chomping on toast and peanut butter fingers. Most of the peanut butter was spread over his face, hands, and tray by the look of him. "Babysitting all day."

"If you have to stay with the bairn, I'll keep you company."

"Thanks." She tried to inject some enthusiasm into her voice. They had been best friends forever. She enjoyed his company, but she hoped to see something of Daniel this weekend. Last Saturday and Sunday, she and Lyall had gone away to a mutual friend's wedding. Add in the evening surgeries she'd been stuck with when a colleague was sick, and she had seen little of Daniel these last two weeks.

Her gaze drifted to the door to the hall for the umpteenth time, eager for him to come down.

"The Sassenach major is not for you, Meg."

Lyall's uncompromising tone snapped her attention back to him. "Says who?"

"Have you not seen the articles on the Internet about him? He likes fast cars and fast women. He'll not settle down here with you, lass."

"When I want your opinion on the matter, Lyall Stewart, I'll ask for it." Megan banged about, taking her irritation out on the cast iron skillet as she turned the bacon, sausages, and haggis. What annoyed her most was that Lyall had voiced her own fears.

The sound of a door shutting upstairs carried into the kitchen, followed by the faint thump of footfalls on the stairs.

Lyall put his cup on the counter. "Think I'll be on my way. I've just remembered something I want to do."

"What about your breakfast?" Megan nodded towards the pan.

"I've lost my appetite." With an unreadable glance, Lyall stomped out the back door.

What was eating him? Megan stared after him for a moment, puzzled, then turned as Daniel strolled through the door, his usual grin in place.

The dogs jumped up, tails wagging, and wriggled around his feet, vying for attention. "Hey there, Bruce, hey, Torrie. Are you good boys?" Daniel patted them and stroked behind their ears.

Megan's heart did a happy jig, her pulse rate increasing at the sight of him.

The dogs went back to their beds in the corner and Daniel turned his attention to Megan. "Good morning, stranger. I've missed you this week."

"I had to cover evening surgery at short notice. A bit of a pain."

Fergus bounced in his high chair, slapping his palms on his tray, squealing with excitement.

"How are you, Gussy? Wearing your breakfast, I see," Daniel said.

"Dan, build. Dan, build." Gus pointed at the wooden bricks on the floor.

Daniel picked up a few and built a tower on the table.

"Gus wants." Fergus bounced some more.

"I think Auntie Meg would like to wipe those dirty fingers before you touch anything, bud."

To distract him, Daniel grabbed a toy dog and bounded it around the table, making it snuffle and bark. Fergus giggled while Bruce and Torrie jumped up from their spot in the corner and joined in the racket.

It seemed her nephew and the dogs had also fallen under Daniel's spell. Everyone seemed to like him except for Lyall and Angus, but then Angus didn't like anyone much.

Megan laughed, the atmosphere in the room lighter now Daniel had arrived to lift Lyall's gloomy cloud.

"I hope you're hungry. There's lots to eat."

"Ravenous. Can't beat a Kindrogan Scottish breakfast, cooked by the fair hand of the laird's daughter."

Megan blushed, more at his intonation than his words, and the way his eyes twinkled with memories of their kiss. She had thought about that kiss a lot. Lyall was no doubt right; Daniel was only passing through. She already knew that in three weeks he would fly to Norway for cold weather training with the army. He might then return to the institute, or he might be posted overseas.

If she wanted to spend time with Daniel, she must

take her chance while he was here. With two brothers and a father in the army, she knew that army doctors had to go where they were sent. Wives and girlfriends came in second place.

Daniel sat beside Fergus, seemingly unconcerned by the sticky fingers waving dangerously close to his oatmeal-colored cable-knit sweater.

He was not the shallow pleasure-seeker that the news reports and pictures suggested. There was so much more to Daniel than that. She was certain.

Megan set a huge plate of breakfast before him of fried eggs, haggis, sausages, bacon, potato scones, fried tomatoes, and mushrooms.

"Wonderful. You cook the best breakfasts." He tucked in with relish, giving a little groan of appreciation that made her knees weak.

"Lyall's mother taught me. She's our housekeeper. She's a lovely woman. It's a shame she's not here at the moment." Megan set her own plate on the table and sat down.

"I thought I might go on a tour of the local area today. Maybe have lunch out. Would you like to join me?" Daniel said.

If Mrs. Stewart were here to look after Fergus, Megan would jump at the chance. "I'm babysitting all day, I'm afraid."

"Bring Fergus." Daniel tapped the end of the baby's nose, making him giggle. "You'll enjoy a day out, won't you, Gus?"

Daniel's gaze moved back to Megan and her heart skipped a beat as their eyes met. What was it about this man that arrowed right to the core of her being? She'd never felt anything like it before.

"Sean and Kelly have baby carriers to go on their backs. Does Hew have something like that?" he asked.

"Yes. It's at his cottage."

"Can we pick it up on the way out? I don't mind

carrying Gus."

Megan would take lots of photos of Daniel hiking with a baby on his back and post them on her Facebook page. This kind, friendly man was the real Daniel, not the Romeo who had dated so many glamorous women. If she wished hard enough, she would make that true.

Chapter Seven

Daniel turned the Kindrogan Estate's pickup into the lane where Megan pointed and stopped beside Hew's stone cottage on the banks of Loch Kinder. He leaned forward, hands resting on top of the steering wheel, and took in the view.

A vast expanse of water lay in front of them, as smooth and shiny as polished steel. Mist draped the pine-clad slopes of the mountains on the other side, drifting in ragged wisps like something from a fantasy novel. "What an amazing view," he said softly, more to himself than Megan.

"I'll just run in and find the baby carrier," Megan said. "Won't be long." She jumped out of the passenger's seat and headed for the door on the side of the cottage, her ponytail bouncing, her slender, denim-clad legs striding purposefully.

Daniel glanced over his shoulder to see Fergus asleep in his car seat. Climbing out, Daniel pushed the door closed softly and wandered to the edge of the water. He drew in a breath of the peaty air and let it out on a satisfied sigh.

Hew's cottage appealed to him, with its amazing position right on the banks of the loch. He could imagine living here. He'd always thought of himself as a city boy, yet there was a freedom and space in the

Scottish Highlands that gave him room to breathe, room to think.

Up here in the wilds of Scotland, he liked the man he was far more than who he'd been in London. Peace settled inside him as deep and still as the waters of the loch. He felt happier and more settled than he had in a long time. With the company of the right woman, he could grow to love this wild place.

A massive bird with a wingspan of at least six feet angled down out of the heavy gray sky to skim the water's surface, snatching up a fish in its talons. Daniel gasped, fumbling for his phone to snap a picture. By the time he tapped in his password and activated the camera, the bird was a dot in the sky.

Megan stepped out of the cottage, shut the door, and put the baby carrier in the back of the pickup.

"I saw a big bird over the lake. It swooped down and caught a fish." Daniel heard the childish wonder in his voice, but didn't care if he sounded uncool.

Megan walked over and took his arm, staring out across the lake. "That'll be a white-tailed sea eagle."

"This isn't the sea."

Megan laughed as if Daniel had cracked a joke. She leaned her head against his shoulder and he wrapped an arm around her, pulling her close. He was so ignorant of her world yet he wanted to learn.

"Tell me about the bird."

"White-tailed eagles have been extinct up here since about 1900. Hew's working on a program to reintroduce them to Kindrogan."

"Wow." Hew was such a quiet guy, Daniel had almost overlooked him.

"Shall we get going? We can take a scenic drive through the village and over the mountain towards Braemar. There's a nice pub there."

They climbed in the pickup and Daniel drove through the village of Kinder Vale. Megan pointed out the doctor's surgery where she worked, with the police station right beside it. The small gathering of cottages was pretty in a natural way that blended into the landscape.

Following Megan's directions, Daniel took the narrow mountain pass, grateful that a snowplow had been that way before them. Rocky valleys clothed in pines and cloud-topped snowy mountains stretched away in every direction. A man could lose himself up here and never be found again. Or maybe a man could find out who he really was.

Daniel had planned to sweet-talk Megan; instead he fell quiet, awed by the surroundings, comfortable with the silence between them.

They stopped in the village of Braemar at the heart of the Cairngorms National Park, took Fergus out of his car seat, and wandered along the street looking in the shop windows at the traditional Scottish goods until they reached the Thistle Pub. Sitting in front of a roaring log fire, they ate thick vegetable soup and crusty bread, followed by hot chocolate with Scottish shortbread.

Fergus sat on the floor, chewing a crust of chocolate-dipped bread and picking bark off the logs piled next to the fireplace, making a mess on the carpet. Daniel watched the curious little boy with a warm glow of pleasure that had more to do with the company than the fire. A few months ago, he would never have guessed he'd enjoy a day out like this.

Fergus tossed his crusts in the fire and a smell like burning toast filled the room.

"Oops," Megan said, glancing over her shoulder. "Perhaps we should leave before we get told off."

"Come here, bud. I think we'd better clean you up." Daniel helped Fergus to his feet, brushed the bits off his front, and tidied the mess on the floor.

"You're very domesticated," Megan said.

Daniel laughed. Most of the people he knew would not call him that. He normally left the tidying up to someone else.

They left the pub and headed back to the car.

"It's too snowy up here. Let's go back to Kinder Valley and walk beside the loch," Megan said. "You might catch another glimpse of the white-tailed eagle."

After an uneventful drive back, Daniel parked on the outskirts of Kinder Vale. With much laughing and fumbling, they managed to put Fergus in the baby carrier, then Megan helped Daniel fix it on his back like a backpack.

They wandered along a path beside the loch. Daniel held out his hand and Megan slipped her fingers into his. He squeezed, something inside him clicking into place with a sense of rightness he'd never felt before. It was as if he'd suddenly discovered a new side of himself and it took a little getting used to.

After a while, they sat on a rock side by side staring out over the water. Megan pulled some binoculars from her coat pocket and scanned the loch, then passed them to him, pointing out various landmarks.

Megan was so easy to be with, so relaxing. He could be himself with her and not worry what she thought of him. This must be how it felt to have a wife you knew well and trusted. Marriage and children had never been high on his to-do list, but as he sat there with Megan's hand in his and Fergus warm against his back, the possibility took shape in his mind.

Daniel's search for a more meaningful life had driven him to change his career. Had he been looking in the wrong place for fulfillment? Was he really just missing a family of his own?

Megan carried a tray bearing three mugs of cocoa out of the kitchen and headed for the office along the corridor. She shouldered the door open and smiled at

Duncan as he glanced up.

"Ready for a hot drink?"

"I'm ready for the whiskey you've laced it with." He scraped his fingers through his dark hair and leaned back, taking his cup off the tray and placing it on his desk.

They'd had a quiet Sunday at home. The weather had closed in, bringing a snowstorm, subfreezing temperatures, and a bitter wind. After an early dinner, Duncan retreated to his office, while Daniel helped her clear up in the kitchen and load the dishwasher.

"Dan and I are going to sit in front of the fire in the drawing room. Why don't you join us?"

"I can't. I have things to do."

Megan rested a hand on Duncan's shoulder and glanced at the papers spread over his desk. "What's all this?"

"Hew wants me to look over the grant application for the eagle project."

Poor Duncan worked so hard, with both his role at the army institute and helping Hew manage Kindrogan Estate. He never had a minute to himself. If Megan ever had the opportunity to marry and settle down, she didn't know how she would leave him to cope here. He needed a wife.

"Come on, you can take a break," she encouraged.

"You don't want me cramping your style."

Megan's eyebrows shot up. "What on earth do you think we're planning to do in there?"

"As your brother, I'd rather not know."

"Duncan!"

"Well, you like Daniel, don't you?"

"Yes."

"Good. He's a nice chap and one heck of a surgeon. I leave all the surgery to him nowadays." He patted her hand where it rested on his shoulder. "I hoped you two would hit it off when I introduced you."

"Duncan Mackenzie. Have you been playing matchmaker?"

"I want my baby sister to be happy. Is that a sin?"

Had Duncan really set her up on purpose? Was that why he always backed out of escorting her to the ball each year at the last moment and palmed her off on some poor man who couldn't say no? Megan pressed a hand over her heart, unsure if she should be annoyed or grateful. In the end, gratitude won out. He was only trying to do what was best for her. She looped her arms around his neck and kissed his cheek. He obviously didn't share Lyall's concern that Daniel was the wrong sort of man for her, and she trusted Duncan's judgment.

"Thank you," she whispered. "I do like Dan. I'm not sure I'm quite in his league, though."

"Pfft. You always put yourself down, Meg. You deserve someone to love you."

She hugged him tighter. He could do with a dose of his own advice. She couldn't remember the last time he'd had a date.

She picked up the tray and wandered towards the drawing room with a hint of trepidation. Ever since they'd visited Hew's cottage, Daniel had been quiet and thoughtful. She didn't know what to make of his unusual mood.

Lounging on the sofa, his feet stretched towards the fire, Daniel had his hands linked over his belly. He smiled as she entered and set the tray on a side table.

"Here you are." She passed across a mug of cocoa and claimed her own.

He patted the seat at his side. "Sit with me."

Her heart gave a little bump as she slid onto the sofa beside him, wanting to snuggle up close, yet not confident enough to do so. She couldn't judge where she was with him. Although he seemed affectionate and friendly, he hadn't kissed her yesterday while they were out, or today, even though they'd been alone together and he'd had the chance.

He drew in a breath and blew it out. "I want you to forget what I said after the New Year's ball. I've changed my mind."

For a moment, Megan couldn't draw breath. She wanted so badly to believe he was referring to his relationship comment. "You said you wanted to concentrate on your work."

He shook his head. "I don't think I knew what I wanted."

"And you do now?"

He laughed wryly. "Not really. But I do know I like being with you. I want us to spend more time together."

Turning to face her, he folded a leg between them on the sofa and rested an elbow on the back. "Can we do that, Meg, spend more time together?"

Was the man crazy? Didn't he know how much she liked him? Megan opened her mouth but nothing came out. She had to clear her throat and try again. "Yes."

A smile burst across his face like the sun breaking over a mountain. A sudden bright energy filled the room. "Wonderful." He lifted a hand and cupped her cheek. "I want to be with you, sweetheart. There's something about you that... Let's just say I've never met a woman like you before."

He set his mug on the floor, took hers from her hand, and put it down. Then he leaned close, tenderly stroking strands of hair away from her face.

Instinct took over. Megan reached for him, sliding her arms around his neck to pull him close. He wrapped her in his embrace and their lips met. She sank into the dreamy kiss, her body warm and melting against him. Being with Daniel felt so right, as if he were the man she had been waiting for all her life.

He cuddled her close, stroking her hair. "Oh, Megan, sweetheart."

She loved the feel of him, the smell of him, the sound of his voice. She loved him.

Chapter Eight

Daniel changed into his scrubs, then paused, a hand against the wall, and tried to focus on the operation he was about to perform. Thoughts of Megan filled his head, making it almost impossible to concentrate on work.

She had become the most important thing in his life, pushing work into a distant second place. Every day, he woke early to walk the dogs with her. As dawn broke and the wintry sun cast its rays across the loch, they wandered hand in hand. Then they laughed together as they cooked breakfast. He couldn't bear to be apart from her a minute longer than necessary. He drove her to work and picked her up when his schedule allowed.

All day he looked forward to seeing her again. He escaped from work as early as possible and spent every minute of the evening in her company, helped her prepare dinner, played with Fergus if she were babysitting. He wanted to be with her, hear her soft Scottish accent, smell her floral fragrance, hold her hand, or have his arm around her. If he wasn't in physical contact with her, he ached a little inside.

The rush of pleasure when he saw her face was like nothing he'd ever experienced before. He struggled to make it through the day without her, texting her every spare moment like a teenager, then staring at his phone, barely able to breathe until she replied.

He was going crazy and he didn't know how to handle it.

Gazing at the mirror, he pulled a scrub cap over his hair, noting the dark rings under his eyes from disturbed sleep spent dreaming of Megan.

They had one more weekend together before he left for cold weather training in Norway. He wasn't sure how he would cope spending eight weeks away from her, when he struggled to manage a few hours.

A knock sounded, making him jump.

"Yes," he said.

One of the nurses popped her head around the door. "Kieran Smyth is prepped for surgery, sir."

"Thank you. I'll be right there."

When the door closed, Daniel pressed a hand over his eyes and strove for equanimity. This was only a minor operation. He could do it in his sleep, but he mustn't. For Kieran it was deadly serious. Daniel owed his patient absolute concentration.

He headed along the corridor towards the operating room. He scrubbed up and a nurse helped him into his gown and gloves, then held the door open for him.

Kieran lay on the operating table with machinery beeping around him. His nervous gaze found Daniel.

"Hello, Kieran. This won't take long. I'll have you back with your mum very soon. Are you feeling okay?"

The boy nodded and Daniel smiled in return.

"Ready, sir," the young anesthetist said. Naomi Gray was a captain recently graduated from the Royal Military Academy Sandhurst. In the past, Daniel would have been charmed by her blonde hair and green eyes, but he didn't feel even a fleeting moment of attraction. Megan swamped every one of his brain cells, leaving no room for other women.

Daniel held Kieran's gaze with a reassuring smile as Naomi injected anesthetic into the cannula in the back of the boy's hand. "Count backward from ten for me, Kieran," she said.

The boy's voice came out as little more than a whisper, fading away at four. Daniel waited while the captain checked some readings.

"Okay," he said. "Let's get started."

Duncan came in masked, but not gloved. "Just going to watch, if that's all right."

"Be my guest." Daniel liked an audience. He actually performed better when he was under scrutiny.

A nurse fitted on his eye loupes. He held out a hand for a scalpel, then carefully pared away the damaged tips of the two fingers, debriding the necrotized tissue to prevent gangrene. The nail had come off the smallest finger as he predicted. He doubted it would grow back. But the nail on the ring finger was intact. When he reached healthy tissue, he stitched the wounds, keeping the stitches small so the scar would be smooth and neat.

He turned to the thumb and cut away the blackened dead flesh and bone.

"Poor, lad," Duncan said.

"He'll be fine." Daniel glanced over his shoulder. "I won't leave him without a thumb."

He picked up the surgical stainless steel bone screw from the dish a nurse offered him. He drilled a hole in the metacarpal bone and cemented the post in, taking care to ensure it was the right length.

He had marked out a rectangle of tissue on the boy's forearm before he started. Now he cut it away with the ease of experience, folded it over the metal post and stitched it in place, working to form it into a thumb shape that would match the other hand.

When he'd finished, he lifted the hand by the wrist and turned it, checking his work from all angles. "I think that's acceptable." He glanced over his shoulder at Duncan. "All right with you?"

Duncan's eyebrows rose. "Excellent result. Well done."

"Dress the wounds, please." With a nod to the team, Daniel headed back to the scrub room, Duncan at his side. As soon as they were alone, Duncan tossed his mask in the bin and shook his head. "You're killing me here, Fabian. I've been doing this for five years. You started a few weeks ago, and your work is so fast and neat you make me feel like an amateur. I'd have taken twice as long and not produced such a good outcome."

Daniel stripped off his gloves and dumped his gown in the laundry bin. "I've heard it said that if you do anything for ten thousand hours you become an expert. I'm not sure I've spent that long performing surgery, but working in my father's clinic gave me the opportunity to operate more often than you will have done here, and the procedures were far more complex and challenging than Kieran's hand."

Daniel pushed open the door and led the way into the corridor. Even as he talked to Duncan, in the back of his mind he was counting down the minutes until he could leave to see Megan. "I've just had more practice than you."

"You're also very diplomatic." Duncan laughed wryly. "Me and my big clumsy fingers aren't really cut out for surgery. I'd better get some paperwork done. See you later."

Daniel headed for his office, stepped inside, and rested his back against the door. He liked Duncan a lot. He got on well with the guy, but he really wanted some time alone with Megan. He had taken things slowly, but he badly wanted to make love with her before he left for Norway. The first time they spent the night together, he did not want her brother sleeping a few doors down the corridor. That was bound to cramp his style.

He grabbed his phone from the desk drawer where he'd left it. A text from her flashed on the screen. How did it go with Kieran?

Good! he texted back. Would you like to come to Edinburgh with me for the weekend?

He stared at the screen, his heart thumping like a schoolboy, counting the seconds until she replied.

Yes!

He grinned so wide, his face hurt.

Megan snuggled up to Daniel's side in the back of the cab as it wove through the Edinburgh traffic, taking them back to their hotel. They had arrived on the train that morning, dropped their bags at the hotel, and spent the day sightseeing. Because Megan studied medicine at Edinburgh University, she knew the city well. She'd given Daniel a tour of some of her old haunts, as well as visiting the medieval fortress dramatically situated on its rock above the city.

The black cab stopped outside the hotel with a screech of brakes. Daniel paid the driver, then they climbed out and walked hand in hand through the sliding doors.

At the check-in desk, Daniel filled out the guest information form. "I hope you enjoy your stay," the receptionist said, handing them two plastic key cards.

They'd lunched at a small bistro tucked among the narrow medieval streets of the old town, a place Megan had frequented when she was a student. She hadn't managed to eat much, though. A shimmering bundle of excitement and nerves filled her stomach. They'd had a wonderful time sightseeing, but she knew why Daniel had brought her to Edinburgh. It had nothing to do with the beautiful castle.

Megan trembled with anticipation as they climbed in the elevator. She couldn't wait to spend the night in Daniel's arms.

He squeezed her hand. "Cold?"

She flashed a smile and nodded, unwilling to reveal

how nervous she was. The fear she might fall short of the bevy of beauties he'd dated lay like a lump of cold porridge in her stomach.

They walked out on the top floor and wandered along the corridor to their room. Daniel released her hand to push in the key card. He'd hardly let go of her all day, as if he feared she might disappear if he weren't holding her hand.

"Wow! This room is fantastic." Classic dark wood furniture with burgundy and navy drapes, sofa, and carpet gave the room a classy, timeless feel. Megan rushed to the window to stare out at the scenic view across Edinburgh to the castle in the distance. She glanced at the doors leading off the sitting room area and realized this wasn't an ordinary room, it was a suite. She frowned, surprised.

Daniel must have noticed her reaction. He shrugged. "I'd love to share a room with you, but I wanted to give you a choice."

He was always a gentleman, never rushing her into anything she wasn't ready for. Megan appreciated that. She checked inside one bedroom, then crossed the sitting room to pop her head through the door of the other. Both rooms were similar, both luxurious.

Daniel picked up their bags. "Where do you want yours?"

She was looking forward to spending the night with Daniel, but it might be nice to have her own space to change and prepare. "I would like my own room."

Daniel's disappointment hit her like a physical blow. His shoulders slumped, his expression bleak.

She should have explained herself better; the last thing she wanted to do was hurt him. Closing the gap between them, she put her arms around his neck. "Just so I can get ready. I want to spend the night with you."

His grin flashed back, full of relief. "Don't do things like that to me, sweetheart. I nearly had a heart attack."

He dropped the bags and pulled her close, lifting her off her feet as he kissed her. They held each other tightly, his breath warm against her hair.

She had never gone away with a man before and didn't know how to behave. But Daniel wasn't just any man; he was the man she loved. All she had to do was be herself and show him how she felt. She sank into his arms, relishing his hard, muscular body against her.

In a few days, he would leave for Norway. She wanted to hold him and love him and make some memories to keep her warm during the long nights he was away.

"Let's take both bags into one room." Forget the pretty nightdress she had planned to wear. She didn't want to waste time primping. She just wanted to be with Daniel.

"Megan." He stroked back her hair, staring into her eyes, then kissed her so softly and sweetly she nearly melted on the spot.

Megan framed his face between her hands, his expression serious for once, intense, almost vulnerable. "I love you, Daniel," she said against his lips.

He scooped her up in his arms and carried her towards the bedroom, dropping tiny kisses on her eyelids, her nose, and her lips. "I love you too, Megan Mackenzie. I didn't even know what those words meant until I met you."

Once Daniel had held Megan in his arms all night, he couldn't bear the thought of sleeping without her. Back at Kindrogan, he slipped into her room every night and stayed until they rose to walk the dogs.

In the early hours of Thursday morning, Daniel lay beside Megan, watching her sleep. He tried to imprint on his mind this image of her, soft and peaceful. During the cold, lonely nights in Norway, he would remember. His phone was loaded with photographs of her, but there would be times when he didn't have access to power. Then he'd have to depend on his memories and the photograph he'd printed to keep in his pocket.

A door closed outside in the corridor. Daniel stirred, checking the clock. He and Duncan were due to catch the train at six. They needed to leave soon. Reluctantly, Daniel slipped out of the warm bed. He leaned over Megan, breathed in her fragrance, and kissed her cheek. "I'm going to my room to get dressed, sweetheart. I'll come back to say good-bye."

She mumbled and blinked sleepily. A wave of pain passed through him. He pressed his lips to her neck, willing her to understand how he felt. He didn't want to leave her. This time he had no choice. It was too late to back out. He'd made a commitment to the army and to Duncan. But he would not leave her again.

If the army decided to post him overseas, he would resign. They needed him more than he needed them. With his experience, he could easily find another job. He liked working for the army, but not if it meant being away from Megan. Life was too short to be parted from his most important person.

He strode along the corridor to his cold room and dressed quickly in winter uniform, only vaguely aware of his belongings lying around—his Rolex watch, his snowboard, his designer gear that had seemed so important to him before.

During the last few weeks, he'd realized the material possessions he'd treasured didn't matter anymore. All that mattered was Megan. When he arrived back from Norway, he planned to sell his London penthouse and swap his sports car for a four-wheel drive.

As he left his room to return to say good-bye to her, Duncan strode towards him. Duncan reached her door first, knocked, and put his head inside. "We're off, Meg. I have my phone if you or Hew need to contact me. Just leave a message and I'll get back to you when I can. I've asked Lyall to keep an eye on things and make sure you're all right."

"Wonderful," Daniel muttered. "Encourage the competition to hang around her, why don't you." If Megan needed help, he wanted her to have it. Not from Lyall, though.

"See you downstairs in ten minutes," Duncan said to him, heading away down the corridor.

Ten minutes! Desperation flashed through Daniel as he slipped into Megan's room and closed the door. How would he survive without her for eight weeks?

He stretched out on the bed at her side, moving the covers off her face so he could see her. She turned into his arms, all warm, sleepy, and adorable, her hair silky and fragrant.

"I don't want to leave you," he whispered.

She burrowed against his chest, curling her fingers in his shirt. "I wish you didn't have to go."

"I love you, Meg. I'll miss you every day." He punctuated his words with kisses.

"I love you, too. Come back to me safe and sound."

"Don't worry. It's only training."

Megan sighed, and seemed to wake up. "Just be careful, Dan. There's always some risk involved in military training."

Her words jolted him. Although he'd joined the army, he'd never considered he'd be in danger. After all, he was a doctor, not a soldier.

Tears gleamed in her eyes and twisted a knife in Daniel's guts. Leaving her was the hardest thing he'd ever done. Why had he joined the damned army? What had he been trying to prove?

A knock sounded on the door. "Time to go, Dan."

Megan huddled close and they kissed. She stroked his cheek, ran her hand over his hair, her eyes scouring his face as if she were memorizing him.

Duncan knocked again. "Come on, Romeo."

"Go," Megan whispered.

Daniel pressed his lips to hers in one last desperate kiss, then scrambled off the bed, backing away, their gazes locked until the last moment. He gripped the door handle and swallowed hard, clearing the tightness from his throat.

Whoever wrote that love hurt was right. He'd never felt this bad in his life before.

Chapter Nine

Lyall poured a cup of coffee and Megan thought she was going to throw up. Ugh, nausea rose in her throat and she felt awful. Tea was her preference, but she normally didn't mind the smell of coffee. Yet for some reason, over the last few days she'd really gone off it.

She turned the sausages, bacon, and haggis frying in the skillet and held her breath. This didn't smell too good either. Nothing did. Perhaps she was coming down with a bug. These last few weeks she'd felt so tired. She was definitely not herself.

Daniel would be home in a couple of weeks and she really wanted to be fit and healthy to greet him. Ever since he left, she'd been looking forward to his homecoming. The last six weeks apart from him had been the longest of her life. She couldn't wait to see his face, hear his voice, snuggle close to him, and feel his strong arms around her.

A lovely gold bracelet had arrived the first week Daniel was away. Every week since then, two jeweled beads had been delivered from him, each package accompanied by a sweet message telling her how much he loved her. The bracelet was so pretty with the beads sparkling in the kitchen lights, each decorated with different colored jewels.

The bracelet was a pleasing weight on her wrist, a

constant reminder of the man she loved. Daniel must have bought it and arranged the delivery before he went away. She had never dreamed he was such a romantic.

Holding her breath, she slid the spatula into the skillet and served up Lyall's breakfast, then handed him the plate. "There you go. Hope you're hungry."

"Wonderful. Thanks. Your breakfasts are as good as Mum's and that's saying something."

He sat down, moving aside the huge vase of flowers Daniel had sent her. This was the third bunch, a beautiful arrangement of exotic blooms delivered from a specialty flower shop in Edinburgh.

Lyall nodded at the vase as Megan joined him at the table with a cup of weak tea, her stomach too sensitive for anything else. "I assume all the flowers mean Fabian is coming back here after his training exercise."

"You assume right." Although she didn't know how long Daniel would be able to stay. Duncan had been posted at the institute for five years now. If Daniel specialized in thermal medicine, there was a good chance he could work in Scotland for the foreseeable future.

Nausea rose in Megan's throat. She took a sip of tea and pressed a hand over her mouth. She really did feel rotten. If they weren't short staffed at the doctor's surgery she might ask for the day off.

"Are you all right, lass," Lyall asked, pinning her with a concerned gaze.

"Not really, but I'll manage. I'll just pop upstairs for a moment before we go."

Megan hurried to her room. She felt so bad, she sat on the edge of the bathtub with her head in her hands for five minutes, sure she was about to throw up. She didn't, but she still felt nauseated.

Checking her watch, she stood with a sigh. She didn't have time to be ill. After splashing cold water on her face and repairing her makeup, she went downstairs, slipped on her shoes, and grabbed a coat before she met Lyall outside.

The four-wheel drive headed towards Kinder Vale, Lyall chatting about some of the problems he was handling. He asked her opinion of Andrew McKay, a teen from a notorious family. They seemed to be the source of all trouble in the village.

Megan struggled to concentrate and answer. In addition to the nausea, her brain felt fuzzy, as if it were full of cotton wool. What was the matter with her? She needed to pull her thoughts together before she saw her patients.

Lyall stopped outside the police station and cut the engine. "You going to be all right, Meg?"

"Yes. I'll be fine. Thanks for the ride. See you later." She climbed out and headed into the small surgery. The receptionist greeted her as she walked through the waiting room. When she reached her consulting room, she hung up her coat and pulled open her desk drawer to put away her handbag. Then she realized she'd forgotten to pick her bag up.

"Darn." She frowned and rubbed her forehead. Perhaps she should have stayed in bed.

"Morning, Meg. How are you?" Gerald, the senior partner of the practice, put his head around her door.

Megan dropped into her chair. "I've been feeling nauseated for a few days. It gets better as the day goes on, then the next morning it's just as bad again. I can't seem to shake it off."

"You're not pregnant, are you?" Gerald's eyebrows rose and he chuckled at his quip as he wandered away.

Megan froze, her hand against her belly, her mind blanking for a second before racing back over her time with Daniel. She couldn't be pregnant. Could she? They'd taken precautions. Although, as a doctor she knew very well that accidental pregnancies happened all the time.

With an unsteady hand, she grabbed a pregnancy kit from the shelf in her office, hid it under her sweater, and hurried to the bathroom. Ten minutes later she sat back in her office chair, staring at the two pink lines with a sense of unreality.

She was pregnant with Daniel Fabian's baby.

Part of her soared with joy. This was tempered by a horrible fear that Daniel might not be as pleased as she was. After all, they'd only known each other for a few months. Their relationship was still very new.

Glancing down, she placed a hand gently over her belly, a smile pulling at her lips. She was pregnant, something she'd dreamed of. She would be a mum and it was Daniel who'd made this dream come true.

She closed her eyes and imagined herself with her baby in her arms, Daniel at her side, his arm around her shoulders, smiling down at the cute little bundle with his brilliant grin, the grin that filled her with joy every time she saw his face.

He would be happy about the baby; she was certain. She reached for her bag to grab her phone, then remembered she didn't have it. Maybe this was something she should tell him face-to-face, anyway. She couldn't wait for him to come home.

The British troops were stationed at a small port 150 miles north of the Arctic Circle. With deep snow, ice, and temperatures regularly thirty degrees below freezing, the conditions were ideal for testing the men and machinery in extreme cold weather warfare.

In the last seven weeks, Daniel had dug himself a snow cave and spent the night inside it, skied three miles cross-country with his medical pack on his back, practiced ice climbing, and spent cold nights in a two-man tent in the middle of an ice field.

The most fun had been skijoring, being towed on

skis behind a BV-206 all-terrain vehicle. He'd been eager to take part in all the training, thinking it would be great practice for working with the Scottish mountain rescue team.

Gratefully wrapped in thermals and winter uniform, he watched the soldiers practicing the ice-breaking drill. He winced as a young private hardly out of his teens pushed his feet in his ski bindings and slid down into the freezing cold water through an ice hole. This was one exercise he was happy to sit out.

The poor guy panted as the cold water hit his face. Splashing around, he pulled the heavy pack off his shoulder and heaved it onto the ice. His sergeant squatted a few feet away, encouraging him. "Name and number, soldier."

The guy in the water gave the details, then dug the spikes of his ski poles in the edge of the hole, kicked his legs, and pulled himself out. It seemed harsh to practice such a thing when the air temperature was fifteen degrees below freezing, but it taught the men how to get themselves out of trouble if they fell through a hole in the ice.

With his white coveralls clinging to his wet thermals, and his sneakers squelching with each step, the soldier jogged to the makeshift bar a few yards away, toasted the Queen, and knocked back his shot of whiskey. Then he headed to the warm tent where his dry clothes were laid out.

This was where Daniel came in. He and Duncan had to monitor the troops for signs of cold injury. He followed on the man's heels, pulling back the tent flap to be greeted by the welcome warmth.

Duncan was just finishing with the previous soldier, now warmly dressed and sipping a hot drink.

"How are you feeling, Private?" Daniel said, approaching the wet soldier as he stripped off.

"Cold, sir."

They both laughed.

Daniel waited while the man dried himself and pulled on some thermals. "I need to check your hands and feet. Sit down here for a moment."

Daniel indicated a small canvas stool. He sat on another and examined the man's hands for discoloration. This ice-breaking exercise came at the end of a rigorous seven weeks of exposure to subfreezing temperatures. They had already sent two men home and were vigilant for any signs of cold injury. This last exercise might be the final straw for anyone who was already vulnerable.

"Have you suffered any pain, numbness, or tingling in your fingers or hands?"

"No, sir."

They had been testing a new thermal fabric during this training exercise. It was proving to be excellent, thin and stretchy but with a thin layer of vacuum-filled bubbles in the middle that provided insulation. Daniel wore it himself and could attest to its efficacy. He planned to recommend it to Kindrogan Mountain Rescue when he got home.

"Let me see your feet. Right one first, Private."

"Yes, sir." The man lifted his right foot onto the footrest, and Daniel checked it over. He wasn't as happy with the guy's feet. The skin looked discolored.

"Have your feet been hurting?"

The young soldier averted his gaze before he answered. "A little. But I didn't think it was enough to complain about, sir."

"Left foot."

The man swapped the foot on the support. This one was worse, the toes red, the skin shiny and swollen in places. They would be blistering soon.

Daniel glanced around for the new thermal socks the man should be wearing and saw no sign of them. "Where are your insulating socks, Private?"

"They make my feet itch, sir. I did tell the sarge."

Daniel sucked in a breath and released it slowly. "You're given these special socks to wear for a reason. What's your name?"

"Private Montgomery, sir. Call me Monty."

"Well, Monty. It looks like you'll be coming to the Institute of Thermal Medicine with me. Some of your toes have frostbite. You should have come to one of the doctors and reported the discomfort before the ice-breaking drill."

"Sorry, sir."

Daniel shook his head. These young men were so eager to please, they didn't report health issues if it interfered with their training.

"Is it serious, Doc?"

"We won't know for a few weeks. We'll admit you to the ward and keep you under observation." The man's face fell. Daniel felt sorry for him. There was such keen competition between the soldiers. Being sent home for this would earn him a good ribbing by his mates. He called a nurse over to dress the man's feet and went to find Duncan.

He stood near the ice hole. The soldiers waiting to take their turn were lined up to one side. "My last guy has clinical signs of cold injury. I hope it'll heal, but we need to get him in the warmth and keep him there."

"Brigadier Palmer mentioned the air support is heading back to the UK this afternoon. If I can swing it, you could ride back with them and admit the casualty straight away. One of the Sea Kings should be able to drop you at the institute."

Daniel's heart soared. Megan had never been far from his mind. Sitting on his own in his ice cave or huddled in his sleeping bag in a tiny tent, every quiet moment his thoughts turned to her. If he could go home early, it would be fantastic.

"Okay. I'll tell the casualty to prepare, and alert his

commanding officer," Daniel said.

His fingers went to the photograph of Megan in his pocket. His phone battery had died long ago, so he hadn't been able to look at the photos on his phone or contact her for days. But he'd carried her picture with him everywhere.

He couldn't wait to hold her in his arms again.

Chapter Ten

Rain pelted so hard Megan was soaked running the twenty feet to Lyall's vehicle. She jumped in with a shiver and huddled in front of the warm air blower. She was cold and wet, but at least by the time her morning surgery ended, the nausea had subsided. It always faded in the middle of the day, or that had been the pattern over the last few weeks.

Lyall glanced at her as she grabbed a hank of hair and squeezed the rain out onto the floor of his police car. "Are you feeling better today? You've got a bit more color in your face."

She laughed. "I'm fine, thanks." The last few weeks had been awkward between them. She'd kept avoiding Lyall's questions about why she was ill. Normally she confided in him, but Daniel must be the first person to know about the baby.

Lyall revved the engine and pulled away, ducking his head to view the tops of the mountains. Megan followed his gaze. The mountain peaks were obscured by heavy gray clouds, sheets of rain sweeping down the valley.

"I hope this weather doesn't catch anybody out. Don't fancy trekking up there today to pull some climber out of trouble."

Megan didn't either. She'd have to consider when to

suspend her mountain rescue work. She didn't want to put her baby at risk. When Daniel came home, they'd discuss it.

She shivered, not from cold but anticipation. He'd texted her to say he was coming back early with a casualty. By tonight he would be home.

She planned to cook Daniel roast venison. Over a candlelit dinner, she'd break the news of her pregnancy. A twinge of worry hit her but she pushed it aside. Daniel would be pleased about the baby. Every time she imagined his reaction, he grinned his wonderful grin and hugged her.

Rain slashed over the windshield, such a deluge the wipers couldn't keep the glass clear. "Don't you just love Scotland," she said.

Lyall sang a few lines of "Bonny Scotland." Megan joined in and they sang at the top of their voices as they bumped through potholes in the road, unable to see more than a few yards ahead in the awful weather. When they finished, they both burst out laughing.

How she wished she could confide in her friend that she was pregnant. If it were any other secret, she would have told him. She and Lyall had always been close and shared confidences. This was the first time another man had come between them.

They pulled up in the Kindrogan courtyard outside the back door. Megan summoned her strength, then shoved open the car door and dashed through the downpour to reach the warm kitchen.

Standing in a puddle, she shrugged out of her coat and kicked off her sodden pumps. Lyall followed her. While he shook their wet coats out the door, Hew arrived in his Kindrogan Estate Land Rover and ran inside with a sleepy Fergus in his arms.

Megan put on the kettle. She wanted to have a quick lunch so she could get on with preparing for Daniel's return. "Anyone want a sandwich?"

Both men replied in the affirmative as her phone dinged with a text. She pulled it out of her bag and stared at the screen.

Power at last. Charged my phone! Leaving soon. Can't wait to see you tonight. All my love, Daniel.

Megan whooped with joy. She couldn't wait to see him.

Lyall raised his eyebrows. "Who's that from?"

"Daniel's coming back early."

"Don't tell me. Pretty boy has injured himself," Lyall said with a cynical twist of his lips.

"No. He's bringing a casualty to the clinic. I'm getting fed up with your snide remarks, Lyall. What's Daniel ever done to you?"

He stared at Megan for long moments, then shook his head and started unlacing his wet boots.

The kettle boiled, its whistle splitting the awkward silence. Too happy at the prospect of seeing Daniel to be annoyed, Megan's smile flashed back as she returned her attention to her phone. Daniel had sent her a video of him in winter uniform standing beside a helicopter. "Just boarding," he'd said, and showed her a view inside the helicopter. "It's a Sea King. Makes me feel right at home."

She smiled at that, remembering the time he'd accompanied the mountain rescue team.

"Can't wait to see you, sweetheart. I love you." He pressed his lips to the tips of his gloved fingers and blew her a noisy kiss.

Megan's heart fluttered like a trapped bird. She held the phone against her chest and sighed with pleasure. Tonight would be wonderful.

Hew was pouring out the tea, so Megan grabbed the loaf of bread and cut slices. She filled sandwiches, then cut them in quarters and heaped them on a plate. After handing out smaller plates, she sat down and watched Daniel's video again a few times, ignoring the long-suffering glances of the men who had to listen to Daniel's romantic words along with her.

Daniel was coming home and he loved her. That was all that mattered. After watching the cute video, she was even more certain he'd be pleased about the baby. He really was the sweetest, most romantic guy she'd ever met. And he was hers.

A discordant burst of bagpipes music cut into the silence. Lyall dug his phone from his pocket and swiped a hand across his mouth to wipe off crumbs as he glanced at the screen.

"It's Duncan." He frowned and put the phone to his ear.

"Hi, Dunc." He listened for a few seconds, his frown deepening.

Why had Duncan called Lyall instead of her or Hew? The thought flitted through Megan's mind, but she was too preoccupied to wonder for long. After lunch, she would clean her bathroom and change the sheets on her bed. This time, Daniel could share her room.

"You've already called RAF Lossiemouth?" Lyall asked.

Megan's attention snapped to Lyall as his words penetrated her thoughts. "Is this a mountain rescue callout?" she mouthed at Hew. He shrugged.

Lyall nodded to himself. "Okay. We'll prepare. I'll keep you posted."

Slipping his phone back in his pocket, Lyall glanced at Hew, his expression guarded.

"Was that a callout?" Megan asked.

Lyall scraped back his hair.

"Lyall." There was something about the grim set of his mouth that made Megan uneasy. "Why did Duncan call you?"

"They've lost contact with the helicopter Daniel's flying back in."

Fear slashed along Megan's nerves. Her hand

clenched reflexively, scrunching her napkin.

"Where? When?"

"About fifteen minutes ago, over the Cairngorms."

Suddenly it all made sense. Duncan had called Lyall to mobilize the mountain rescue team.

A tiny whimper escaped her lips and she pressed a hand over her mouth. This couldn't happen. She couldn't lose Daniel. She tried to summon positive thoughts, tell herself he would be all right, but people died in the Scottish mountains every year. If his helicopter had crashed in the bad weather, his chances were slim.

She jolted to her feet, her chair scraping back with a sickening squeal. "I'll change. We need to leave."

Lyall came around the table and tried to put his arm around her. "It's not a good idea for you—"

She sidestepped, throwing up a hand to hold him off. "Stop it. I'm coming. This is not up for discussion."

There was no way on earth she would stay here when Daniel might be on the mountainside hurt. If he was lost out there, she would find him or die trying.

Daniel spluttered in the cold water. Why had they made him do the ice-breaker drill? He was cold and wet, his thermals clinging to his skin. His head throbbed when he tried to move, and his leg was trapped in the ice.

He was going to drown.

Panicking, he struggled, thrashing his head from side to side, trying to breathe.

Then he came to.

Freezing water beat against the side of his face, trickling into his ear and down his neck.

Where the hell was he? Slitting his eyes open, he saw twisted gray metal with mist swirling past, and rain— heavy, incessant rain mixed with hailstones.

This wasn't the ice hole.

For a moment, relief rushed through him. Then he

remembered: thick clouds, zero visibility, buffeting wind, the pilot fighting for control, then the helicopter crashing, careening along on its side like a crazy fairground ride, equipment tumbling around, banging into him. He must have been knocked out.

Daniel dragged in a breath and released it, the sound emerging as a shivery groan. He lifted a hand to his head, relieved that he could, and touched the throbbing ache above his right ear. With his gloves on, he couldn't determine how bad the injury was.

"Major Fabian, can you hear me?"

Lucidity returned fast now. Daniel held a forearm over his face to shield his eyes from the icy rain and peered towards the voice. The pilot leaned through a gap in the twisted wreckage, blood pouring from a wound on his head.

Daniel grabbed something sturdy beside him and used it to help himself sit up. Pain screamed inside his head. He had to close his eyes and concentrate on breathing until the discomfort subsided. He wiped a glove over his face and it came away bloody. Running his hand over his face again, he searched for the injury. His whole head throbbed, but he located the source—a laceration in his hairline.

"Can you get up, Major?" The pilot called to him again. "I need medical help over here for the copilot."

Daniel had to swallow and suck in a couple of breaths before he could answer. "I'm trying." There was something on top of him. He shoved aside a box and some packs that lay on his legs to reveal a metal girder angled out from the misty gray mass of the wreckage, pinning his left shin.

He shoved at it. Pain ricocheted up his leg and blasted the air from his lungs, leaving him panting. Unless the pilot could shift the girder, he wasn't moving anywhere.

"I'm pinned down," he shouted, hating the feeling of

helplessness.

"Okay. I'll come and help you. Give me a moment."

Dizziness swirled in Daniel's head. With a groan, he lowered himself back down and threw an arm over his face. Clean mountain air filled his nose, then the acrid tang of aviation fuel. At least the temperature and heavy rain would cool any hot metal likely to ignite the flammable liquid.

Metal groaned and clanged in counterpoint to the incessant drumming of rain on the helicopter's hull as the pilot pushed through the wreckage. When the man arrived, Daniel noticed his arm tied against his chest in a blue sling and a bleeding gash across his forehead. His medical training kicked in; for a little while he forgot his own situation.

"Did you lose consciousness?" Daniel asked, wondering if the guy had a skull fracture.

"No. Wish I had. Hurts like blazes."

"What's your copilot's condition?"

"Unconscious but breathing."

"How's the patient I'm traveling with, Private Montgomery?"

"I can't find him."

Daniel sat up again, wincing as the pain in his head flared. He scanned the area for signs of Monty. Through the haze of pelting rain and mist, he could see nothing but twisted wreckage and debris.

"Monty," he called at the top of his voice, gritting his teeth at the resulting head pain.

No answer.

"I only had a quick look outside. I didn't want to leave Frank for too long." The pilot gestured in the direction he'd come.

"We need to move this metal bar that's trapping my leg so I can search for Monty." Pain pounded through Daniel's skull even harder at the thought he'd lost his patient. He prayed the young man was all right.

The pilot kicked away some more debris to give himself space, then using his good arm, he tugged at the fallen girder ineffectually. He shook his head. "I'm not going to move this on my own. You'll have to wait until the cavalry arrives."

"Did you radio for help?"

"The local mountain rescue group is on the way."

"Where did we come down?"

"Cairngorms."

They were near Kindrogan. Megan might be with the rescue team. Her smiling face filled Daniel's mind and hope pulsed through him. He wanted to see her so badly, it brought tears to his eyes.

Chapter Eleven

Conditions were treacherous. Visibility down to a few yards. Megan peered into the mist and picked her way over slippery rocks, fists clenched in her gloves, muscles taut and teeth gritted. She moved as fast as she could, bending into the gale-force winds.

A punishing mix of snow, hailstones, and freezing rain whipped around her as if trying to drive her back. She paused to wipe her goggles and pull the scarf higher over her face before she pushed on.

When she heard Daniel's helicopter had come down, she bottled up her emotions and slapped on a lid. She couldn't let herself feel or she would fall to pieces. That was not an option. Daniel needed her. He was out here waiting for her and she wouldn't let him down. The fear he might be dead nipped at the edges of her mind, but she refused to believe she would lose him.

She lost her footing on loose rocks, going down on her knees. Flanking her silently, like self-assigned bodyguards, Lyall and Hew each put a hand beneath her arms and pulled her to her feet. Once she made it clear she was coming, neither of them had argued. They'd simply stayed with her, watching out for her.

After brushing herself off, she pressed on, breath short in the thin air, muscles burning with effort, maintaining a punishing pace. Most of the team had fallen behind. Even with their high-visibility jackets and flashlights, she couldn't see them anymore. Only Lyall and Hew kept up.

Lyall tapped her arm and gestured for her to stop while he pulled the GPS tracker out of its case. The three of them crowded around it, squinting at the illuminated display. Lyall raised a hand and they headed the way he indicated. They were nearly there.

Through the low cloud and torrential rain, a light waved in the distance. "Look," she shouted to be heard over the howling wind.

There had been four men in the helicopter, so the mountain rescue team had brought four stretchers. They'd even borrowed the all-terrain Sno-Cat with caterpillar tracks from Glenshee to carry the casualties back, if necessary. The vehicle had to drive a longer way around than they had walked. Lyall had wanted her to ride in it, but she was determined to be the first to reach Daniel.

With renewed determination, Megan jogged forward against the wind, her heart pounding with a potent mix of hope and fear. Someone was waving that light. It might be Daniel!

As they approached, a man's form resolved out of the murk. One glance at his silhouette told her it wasn't Daniel. The shock of disappointment nearly took the feet from under her.

Behind the figure lay the uneven, dark bulk of what must be the helicopter wreckage.

"Hello," Lyall yelled over the wind.

"Thank God. It's good to see you." The man stepped back into the relative shelter of the battered metal carcass.

Megan's glance swept over him, an immediate professional assessment of his condition second nature. His arm was in a sling and he had a laceration on his forehead, but he was walking wounded, lucid and alert. "Where's Major Fabian?" she shouted, her heart thumping so hard she could hardly draw breath to speak.

"In here." The man turned and stepped farther inside the wreckage, leading the way. "My copilot is still in the front and we lost a man as we came down."

Megan heard his words but they slid over the surface of her mind, barely registering, her gaze glued on the prone figure a short distance away. She stumbled and slithered over bits of crumpled helicopter, ripping off her goggles, desperate to see Daniel. She fell to her knees at his side, a sixth sense confirming that this was the man she loved before she saw his face.

"Daniel!"

She leaned down and his arms wrapped around her awkwardly as they were both bundled in thick clothes. She buried her face against his chilled cheek, a hint of his familiar fragrance surviving the cold, wet conditions.

For long moments she clung to him, unable to do anything except fight the tears of relief that threatened to burst free.

"I love you." She pressed her lips to his ear, whispering through her tight throat.

"Sweetheart, I'm so relieved to see you. I knew you'd come."

She swallowed hard. Got herself under control. "Are you hurt?"

"My head and shin."

"Your head?" With frantic fingers, she pulled her medical pack off her back and unclipped it. She dug around for wipes and cleaned the blood and dirt from his skin, her gaze scouring his beloved face for injuries. The laceration on his forehead was nothing serious. She ripped off her gloves, and gently felt through his hair.

A nasty lump had come up above his ear, but it didn't appear serious. Her breath leaked out in a gust of relief. She pressed her lips close to his ear. "Minor contusion above your right ear and laceration to your forehead that will require stitching. Nothing to worry about."

"Good." His eyelids fell, and fear spurted through her.

"Daniel, stay with me." She cupped her hand around his cheek.

"My head hurts."

"Hold tight. I'll give you a shot in a moment." She sat back on her heels to examine his body. There were no obvious injuries. The only problem appeared to be a metal girder bent at an angle, trapping his lower leg.

Her gaze rose to find Lyall standing nearby with Hew. "We need to free Daniel," she said.

Lyall nodded. He and Hew tried to lift the metal bar, putting their backs into it. The thing didn't shift. "We'll get the others to help," he shouted.

Megan gripped Daniel's hand, not wanting to leave him, but she was the doctor on the team and there were other casualties.

"The copilot's in the cockpit." The pilot waved his arm to indicate where.

She leaned down, put her mouth to Daniel's ear. "I've got to treat the others."

"I'll be okay. You go," Daniel said. As she drew back, he grinned. Not quite his usual megawatts smile, but so familiar it clenched her heart.

Tears flooded her eyes and she wiped them away. She had to hang on to her composure until this was over. Climbing between the twisted pieces of metal and scattered equipment, she followed the pilot to find a man still strapped in the copilot's chair. His head lolled to the side, but there was no obvious sign of injury.

She took his vitals. "Has he regained consciousness at all?"

"No." She checked him over and found a bump on

his head, but apart from that he had escaped with little obvious physical damage.

"We'll get him loaded on a stretcher and into the hospital. They can do further tests to find out why he hasn't regained consciousness. You mentioned a fourth man?"

"We must have lost him sometime during the crash."

Miraculously the helicopter windshield had survived, cracked but intact, providing a measure of protection from the weather. She stared out at the hailstones running down the glass in the deluge. If the fourth guy was outside in this weather, probably injured, he would die if they didn't find him soon.

"Some men will come with a stretcher and load your copilot. Stay with him for the moment."

She headed back through the obstacle course, noticing the deepening gloom as dusk fell. Night came early in this sort of weather.

"We need to get moving before dark falls," Lyall said as she neared him.

"Have the rest of the team arrived? I want to lift the metal bar off Daniel's leg."

Megan's gaze went to Daniel, to the blue eyes she loved so much. Even here in this terrible situation, he still managed to buoy her spirits. Despite the circumstances, her heart leaped and bounded. He might be hurt but he would be all right.

She crouched at his side, taking the hand he held out. The rest of the team arrived and a group of men heaved the metal girder off his shin, the wrecked helicopter creaking and groaning as it shifted.

She checked his tibia and judged it might be fractured, so she braced it. They wrapped him in thermal blankets and strapped him onto a stretcher. The copilot was also loaded onto a stretcher and carried out.

Lyall sent a team to search the trail the helicopter

had scraped over the ground, looking for the fourth man.

The Sno-Cat arrived and they loaded the two stretchers on the front. The pilot sat inside the cab with the driver.

"You head back to the helicopter pickup point," Lyall said. "I'll stay here for thirty minutes and continue searching. Then we'll walk out before it gets too dark. The helicopter can come back for us. If we find the fourth man, we'll stretcher him out by hand."

Megan nodded. She handed across her medical pack. Lyall wasn't a doctor, but he had thorough first aid knowledge. All the mountain rescue team did.

She stepped up onto the front of the Sno-Cat beside Daniel's stretcher, and hung on as the vehicle bumped and slithered over the terrain. It wasn't designed as an ambulance, but it was all they had. Leaning over Daniel where he lay bundled under warm blankets, protected from the weather, she pressed her lips to his cold mouth, and stroked his wet hair.

Love you, love you, love you. The words repeated inside her head like a mantra in time with the beat of her heart. She was so relieved to have him back.

Daniel drifted in and out of sleep, vaguely aware of the jostling, bumpy ride on the Sno-Cat. Megan leaned over him, her fingers clenched around his, her warm breath against his cheek, her soft voice in his ear, whispering words of love and encouragement.

In the past, he'd never have relaxed and been comfortable putting his safety in the hands of a woman he was dating. He didn't have much choice right now, but he trusted Megan. He didn't mind her seeing him vulnerable like this.

He slept for a while and woke as they lifted him into the helicopter. Voices spoke over him, packs were dropped on the floor close by, and the familiar smell of aviation fuel tinged the air. Then the door slammed and the floor vibrated beneath him as the helicopter took off.

For a few minutes he couldn't settle, his head pounding again, his shin aching, the pain streaking up his leg even though he'd had a pain relief shot. Then Megan clasped his hand. At her touch, the tension leaked from his body and the pain eased.

They arrived at the hospital to blissful warmth and dry clothes. Megan stayed with him while he was x-rayed, and had his leg strapped up and the wound dressed.

As he was wheeled back along the corridor to his room, the message came through that Lyall had found Monty and he was okay. They were on their way to the hospital. Finally Daniel could relax.

Megan plumped his pillows and gently examined the contusion on the side of his head. "I'm going to leave this uncovered for the moment. The skin is hardly broken."

Daniel didn't care as long as she stayed with him. She sat on a chair beside his bed, still in the thermal undershirt and waterproof trousers she'd worn for the rescue. Her hair was tied back, wisps escaping to frame her face in soft red waves. Her mascara had run, leaving black streaks underneath her eyes, and dirt smudged her cheeks. But her brown eyes glowed with love and she had a permanent smile on her lips.

She was the most beautiful woman he'd ever seen. He never wanted to be parted from her again.

During the lonely nights in his tent, he'd run through numerous ways of proposing to her, trying to think of the most romantic. Lying injured in a hospital bed while she cared for him was nowhere on that list.

She smoothed his pillow and kissed him. "Do you want anything to eat?"

"No. I want to marry you."

Her eyes widened, and she gasped. "Yes, oh yes. I want to marry you, Dan." She pressed her lips to his, then kicked off her boots and stretched out beside him, snuggling into his arms.

"What about the no-visitors-on-the-bed rule?" he said.

"Forget it. I'm your doctor. I prescribe hugs and kisses, Major Fabian."

He caught a strand of silky red hair between his fingers, and savored its texture before stroking it back behind her ear. A few months ago, he couldn't imagine being in love; now he was going to get married. How his life had changed. "So, how soon do you want to set the date?"

"Quickly might be a good idea."

"Why quickly?"

"I'm pregnant."

For a moment, Daniel's mind blanked with disbelief before he found his tongue. "How?"

"You must have bumped your head harder than I thought if you need to ask that."

He chuckled and pulled her closer. Images of Megan with his baby in her arms filled his mind, images of the three of them living together as a family. This was what he wanted, what he'd been missing. No wonder Sean was so happy. He'd already discovered this secret.

"I joined the army because I was searching for something more. Yet it was you I needed. You've given meaning to my life, sweetheart."

"So, you're pleased about the baby?" The slight hint of doubt in her voice made him kiss her soundly to reassure her.

"I couldn't be happier. Fate was smiling on me the day I met you."

"I think Duncan might have had something to do with it."

"I'll have to thank him then."

"What about a summer wedding?" Megan suggested. "Darling, I can't wait."

Chapter Twelve

Megan gazed out her bedroom window at the people gathered on the lawn by the loch, ready for her wedding. The sun shone out of a cerulean sky, golden sunlight playing across the rippling water. An aisle ran between neat rows of chairs trimmed with Mackenzie tartan sashes to a heather-covered arch where the vicar stood.

Despite the beautiful view along the valley framed by majestic mountain peaks, it was the small group of people chatting with the vicar who captured her gaze. Daniel's father and mother had surprised him by coming together, and she could tell he was relieved.

Daniel stood with them, tall and stylish in morning dress, his blond hair gleaming in the sunshine. None of the other men could hold a candle to him. Everyone raved about his brother Sean's looks, but Daniel was far more handsome.

"Will you stop staring at your husband-to-be and come here so we can fit your veil? You've got the rest of your life to ogle him," Megan's mother said.

"What a wonderful thought." Megan dreamily dragged her gaze away from the window.

With her mother stood Olivia and Alice Knight and Kelly Fabian, all dressed as matrons of honor in long green satin dresses trimmed with Mackenzie plaid. Daniel's little nieces, Zoe and Annabelle, both dressed in matching flower-girl dresses with plaid bows in their golden hair, sat side by side on the end of the bed, sorting through Megan's jewelry box and trying everything on.

It had taken a wedding to tempt Megan's mother back from Barbados, but it was wonderful to have her home. Slim, elegant, and tanned, her red hair twisted up on her head in a simple chignon with a turquoise fascinator on the side of her head to match her stunning dress, she stood beside Megan in front of the mirror. She attached the veil, carefully rearranging the long ringlets of Megan's hair over her shoulders.

Alice stood on her other side, grinning, while Olivia and Kelly looked on from behind them, both a head taller than Alice, Megan, and her mother.

The translucent veil sprinkled with pearls draped over Megan's bare shoulders, the effect pleasing. The scalloped sweetheart neckline of her strapless wedding dress showed off the diamond and pearl necklace Daniel had given her.

She smiled, satisfied with how she looked. In the past, she'd lacked confidence in her appearance. Since she met Daniel, she saw herself through his eyes, and her confidence had blossomed. If he thought she was beautiful, she wasn't going to argue.

Embroidery, and pearls to match the veil, decorated the bodice of her gown. The skirt flared out from an empire waistline over full gauze petticoats, the style hiding her burgeoning waistline. The weeks had flown past. She was already nearly six months pregnant, and she couldn't be happier.

Daniel had bought a house at the far end of Loch Kinder on the outskirts of the village. After three months of remodeling, the place was ready for them to move into after the wedding. The only room left to decorate was the nursery. They wanted to do that together now that the builders had finished.

Megan's mother put her arm around her shoulders. "You look stunning, darling. I'm so happy for you. Now we just have to find three nice girls for your brothers." She cast a longing gaze at the other women. "It's a pity you three are already married. You would be perfect for my boys."

A knock sounded on the door. Olivia paced across the room and cracked it open. "This is a testosterone-free zone," she said in a teasing voice, but she stepped back and opened the door.

Lyall came in, handsome in his dark jacket and red Stewart plaid kilt with a metal- and fur-trimmed sporran hanging over the front.

"Lyall." Megan grinned and rushed to him, throwing her arms around his neck. After the rescue, he'd had a complete change of heart about Daniel. She didn't know what had altered Lyall's opinion, but she welcomed the friendship that was growing between her fiancé and her best friend.

"I wanted to give you this." Lyall dug a traditional claddagh brooch out of his pocket and laid it on his palm. "They say a bride should have something old, something new, something borrowed, and something blue. Well, this is something old. It belonged to my grandmother."

"Oh, Lyall. It's beautiful." The round motif with two hands holding a heart topped by a crown was decorated with an intricately engraved Celtic design. It was an ancient symbol of love, loyalty, and friendship—still very much part of the Scottish tradition.

She took it and turned it in her hand, watching the sunlight glitter off the polished silver. She stood on tiptoe and kissed his cheek, holding on tightly and closing her eyes. He'd been there for her all her life. She loved him as much as her brothers.

"I'll treasure it," she whispered.

He nodded. Clearing his throat, he took it back to

pin it on the Mackenzie tartan bow around her wrist. "I'll be watching to make sure that Sassenach takes good care of you, lass, or he'll answer to me."

Megan laughed. "He'll take care of me. You needn't worry about that."

Another knock sounded on the door and Lyall backed away. "I'll leave you in peace." He nodded to the group. "Ladies."

As he left, her father came in, clad in army dress uniform with a Mackenzie plaid kilt. "Are you ready, lass?"

"That I am, sir."

"Then we better not keep the rabble waiting." He poked out an elbow for her to put her hand through. "Shall we?"

Megan rested her hand on his forearm. With her mother and her friends following, she walked beside her father down the wide staircase, past the paintings of generations of Mackenzies who had no doubt trodden this same stairway on the way to their weddings.

"Major Fabian seems like a decent chap," her father said.

"I'm glad you approve."

He nodded. "George Knight likes the lad, so I take that as adequate recommendation."

They paused in the entrance hall while Olivia and her mother arranged the train on her dress and Alice adjusted her veil. Kelly stood directly behind her with Zoe and Annabelle. At the last moment, she handed the children their tartan-trimmed flower baskets of heather.

Hew, Duncan, and Blair stood in the doorway waiting for her, with little Fergus looking adorable, dressed in a kilt, holding his daddy's hand.

"Everyone's ready," Duncan said.

"You're a bonnie bride, Meggie Mackenzie." Blair

winked. "It looks like Fabian got his three thousand pounds' worth that he paid for you at the auction."

"Blair!" She slapped his arm and he grinned at her, unabashed.

Hew signaled out the doorway and the bagpipes started playing. Unexpected nerves tangled inside her.

Duncan smiled, steady and reassuring. "Enjoy your day," he said.

To the poignant strains of "Highland Cathedral," she walked sedately down the flagstone path, through the gate, and onto the neatly-trimmed grass.

Grinning, Daniel stood with his brother, framed by the heather-trimmed arch, Loch Kinder in the background. All her nerves evaporated as she met his gaze. Her spirit soared up to the mountain peaks to think she would soon be married to this wonderful man who had made her feel beautiful and wanted.

Her father shook Daniel's hand, then stepped aside. She passed her bouquet to Alice, slid her fingers into Daniel's, and they turned to face the vicar.

The next half hour passed as if in a dream, her focus completely on Daniel. She barely noticed their friends and family as she repeated the words of the marriage service.

"I now pronounce you husband and wife. You may kiss the bride," the vicar said.

Daniel embraced her and their lips met. For a moment, the world went away. She fell into a blissful place where time stood still. She wasn't alone anymore; they were two, soon to be three. It was the best feeling in the world.

Gasps pulled her back to the moment. Like everyone else gathered there on the lawn that sunny August day at Kindrogan Castle, she shaded her eyes and stared at the white-tailed sea eagle and its two offspring as they skimmed the waters of the loch and glided over the wedding party into the blue sky.

"Magical," Daniel said, craning his neck to follow the birds' path.

He was right. Life was magical with Daniel, and always would be. He'd given her everything she'd dreamed of and thought she would never have. He might be a Sassenach from the wrong side of the border, but he was willing to make his home here in the Highlands of Scotland with her. She couldn't wait for their baby to be born so they could start their life together as a family.

Epilogue

As the final hours of the year ticked away, there was no glamorous ball, sumptuous dinner, or fireworks for Daniel and Megan. Duncan and Blair were in London for the Royal Army Medical Corps New Year's Ball, but inside Eagle Cottage, on the banks of Loch Kinder, the young Fabian family celebrated quietly, content with their own company.

"Here you are, sweetheart." Daniel placed a cup of tea on the nightstand for Megan and climbed into bed beside her. She leaned back on a heap of pillows, breastfeeding their seven-week-old daughter, Heather.

"Thanks. Aren't you going to have a glass of champagne to see in the New Year?" Megan asked.

"As you can't drink at the moment, I thought you might prefer to share these." He laid a heart-shaped box of champagne truffles on the bedspread.

"Oh, Daniel, darling, you are the sweetest man." Megan leaned closer and kissed him.

Gently curving a palm around their daughter's back, he then pressed his lips to his baby girl's forehead. He wanted to hug and kiss his adorable little daughter all the time. He was almost jealous that he couldn't feed her.

He hadn't believed in love at first sight until he glimpsed Heather's squashed face and tuft of red hair.

The first time he held the tiny girl in his arms and stared into her blue eyes, he was a goner.

He wanted nothing more than to spend all his time with his wife and his sweet daughter. Unfortunately he still had to work at the army institute, but not over Christmas and the New Year.

Megan finished feeding Heather. "There you are, my hungry little darling. Daddy's waiting for his cuddle." She passed the baby across.

Daniel took his daughter, cradled her downy head in his hand, and stared at her face, a sense of wonder and love swelling in his chest. "Who's the prettiest baby girl in the world?" He kissed the end of her nose and her cheeks, then held her to his shoulder and rubbed her back to bring up her burps.

Megan finished her cup of tea and put it back on the nightstand with a yawn.

"Are you going to wait up to see the New Year in?" he asked.

"Feed me some chocolates and I'll try to stay awake."

He chuckled as she pulled the wrapper off the box, popped a sweet treat in her mouth, and dimmed the lights.

With Heather cradled in one arm and his darling wife snuggled beneath the other, Daniel relaxed against his pillows, a satisfied sigh whispering between his lips. If someone had told him a year ago that this New Year's Eve he would be married with a baby daughter, he wouldn't have believed them. This was how life should be.

They had installed large windows overlooking Loch Kinder. Their view extended down the valley to the twinkling lights that marked Kindrogan Castle. The full moon glowed in the night sky, casting a rippling trail of silver across the water.

To the gentle music of his baby's breathing and the light display of a trillion stars sparkling in the dark sky,

Daniel watched the clock tick around to midnight.

"Happy New Year, darling," he whispered to his drowsy wife as she stirred against his chest. He kissed her hair, grateful for this wonderful life God had gifted him. "Happy New Year, my precious little girl," he said to Heather.

He had been looking for a new direction and he'd found it. Megan and Heather were his future, the most important things in his life. He'd found the peace and fulfillment he'd been searching for.

His New Year's resolution was easy to choose this year, and it would never change—to love his wife and baby and keep them safe for the rest of their lives.

His darling wife and his New Year's baby were more precious to him than anything else in the world. He planned to spend the rest of his life loving them, and if they loved him half as much, he would be a happy man.

The Army Doctor's Baby

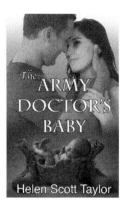

After his wife betrayed him, Major Radley Knight dedicated himself to becoming the best Army doctor he could be, dedicated himself to saving soldiers' lives. When he returns on leave from Afghanistan he is ready for a break. Instead he finds himself helping a young mother and her newborn baby. He falls in love with Olivia and her sweet baby boy and longs to spend the rest of his life caring for them. But Olivia and her baby belong to Radley's brother.

Praise for The Army Doctor's Baby

"This is a sweet romance with a wonderful happily ever after. Highly recommend this read!" Luvbooks

"I loved this sweet, tender romance about a woman in need of a father for her baby and the man who falls in love with her..." Ruth Glick

"Loved the twists at the end of the book. Just the right amount of tension to keep me turning those pages! Totally recommend." Mary Leo

The Army Doctor's Wedding

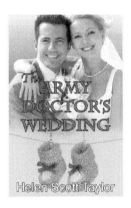

Major Cameron Knight thrives on the danger of front-line battlefield medicine. Throwing himself into saving the lives of injured servicemen keeps the demons from his past away. When he rescues charity worker, Alice Conway, and a tiny newborn baby, he longs for a second chance to do the right thing, even if it means marrying a woman he barely knows so they can take the orphan baby to England for surgery. The brave, beautiful young woman and the orphan baby steal his heart. He wants to make the marriage real, but being married to an army officer who's stationed overseas might do her more harm than good.

Praise for The Army Doctor's Wedding

"Grab a Kleenex because you are going to need it! This is one no romance lover should miss!" Teresa Hughes

"The book starts out with lots of action and holds the reader's interest through to the end. It's a great read!" Sue E. Pennington

The Army Doctor's Christmas Baby

After he loses his wife, army surgeon Colonel Sean Fabian protects his damaged heart by cutting women out of his life. He dedicates himself to his career and being a great dad to his twin babies. When he asks army nurse Kelly Grace to play nanny to his children over Christmas, he realizes how much he misses having a beautiful woman in his life and in his arms. Caring for Sean's adorable twin babies is Kelly's dream come true. She falls in love with the sweet little girls and their daddy, but she's hiding a devastating event from the past. If she can't trust Sean with her secret, how can she ever expect him to trust her with his bruised heart?

Praise for The Army Doctor's Christmas Baby

"...if you want to experience the true essence of Christmas, with the love and understanding that only being with family over the holidays can satisfy, you'll definitely want to experience, The Army Doctor's Christmas Baby." F Barnett

About the Author

Helen Scott Taylor won the American Title IV contest in 2008. Her winning book, The Magic Knot, was published in 2009 to critical acclaim, received a starred review from *Booklist*, and was a *Booklist* top ten romance for 2009. Since then, she has published other novels, novellas, and short stories in both the UK and USA.

Helen lives in South West England near Plymouth in Devon between the windswept expanse of Dartmoor and the rocky Atlantic coast. As well as her wonderful long-suffering husband, she shares her home with a Westie a Shih Tzu and an aristocratic chocolate-shaded-silver-burmilla cat who rules the household with a velvet paw. She believes that deep within everyone, there's a little magic.

Find Helen at:
http://www.HelenScottTaylor.com
http://twitter.com/helenscotttaylo
http://facebook.com/helenscotttaylor
www.facebook.com/HelenScottTaylorAuthor

Book List

Paranormal/Fantasy Romance

The Magic Knot
The Phoenix Charm
The Ruby Kiss
The Feast of Beauty
Warriors of Ra
A Clockwork Fairytale
Ice Gods
Cursed Kiss

Contemporary Romance

The Army Doctor's Baby
The Army Doctor's Wedding
The Army Doctor's Christmas Baby
The Army Doctor's Valentine's Baby
The Army Doctor's Holiday Baby
Unbreak My Heart
Oceans Between Us
Finally Home
A Family for Christmas
A Christmas Family Wish
A Family Forever
Moments of Gold
Flowers on the water

Young Adult

Wildwood

Printed in Great Britain
by Amazon